Ash Gray

Ash Gray

Stay out of the Rockies!

Spartan Lakonian

authorHOUSE®

AuthorHouse™
1663 Liberty Drive
Bloomington, IN 47403
www.authorhouse.com
Phone: 1-800-839-8640

First published by AuthorHouse   07/06/2011

ISBN: 978-1-4634-3062-7 (sc)
ISBN: 978-1-4634-3061-0 (ebk)

Printed in the United States of America

TABLE OF CONTENTS

To my dearest wife, my children, my friends, and also to everyone that has an interest cryptids, phenomena, and other anomalies.

It is my suggestion that when you are in the wilderness or wherever you are, always be prepared for survival!

Foreword

Spartan Lakonian's story brings back memories of growing up in the Pacific Northwest and hearing stories of secretive creatures that might live in the forests. More and more people, in that part of the United States are having eerie experiences or feelings they were being followed or watched while they fished, hiked or hunted. Could something unknown really be lurking in the trees, shadows, or waiting around the bends of the innumerable trails?

We have all woken up terrified from nightmares of dark and shadowy things. Do our minds seem to crave the things of the dark and the things of the unknown? People all over the world have legends of the hidden and the mysterious.

Spartan Lakonian takes us on a journey where Ricky, armed with his shotgun, his courage, his horse, and his hope of survival, comes face to face with his own fear, nightmare, and the unknown.

Marvin Slay Jr.

Preface

I wrote this book to remind people that there are creatures in this world that still remain hidden, but sooner or later, some of those creatures will be discovered. Some of those hidden things live in the deep lakes, the unsearchable depths of the seas, the remote jungles, the uninhabitable Arctic or Antarctic, and some . . . in the woods and mountains of the world.

When we find these new creatures, observe them, photograph them, study them, but most of all . . . respect them!

I want to express my appreciation to my dear wife, my children, and also to Marvin Slay Jr. and Pam Slay, for their enthusiasm in this book. I wish them all the best!

I also want to applaud each researcher in the field of Crytozoology for their labors in bringing to light, the things that hide in the darkness.

Introduction

Many of us, whether we admit it or not, have actually seen something that made us wonder if what we saw was real to begin with. Some of you know what I mean. Some of you may have seen something that broke all the laws of nature, possibility, reality, and even imagination itself.

Some of you want to see that something again and some of you hope that you never, ever, ever, see that something again!

Ricky hoped he would never see that something again, but he soon came to find out that he would, and that there was no way to avoid it!

One cannot always run away from a nightmare . . . because there are some things in this world . . . that are out to get you!

Spartan Lakonian

Chapter 1

Gun Fire

Ranger Ricky Toomis rode slowly along the snowy trail on his dark brown horse named Claire. Ricky Toomis worked for the U.S. Forest Service as a law enforcement officer, in the northern Colorado Rockies. He was single man, with dark brown hair, trimmed mustache, average build, and moderate in height. He didn't speak a lot, but when he did, it was usually important. As a ten year veteran of the U.S. Forest Service, he was living the dream of his life. Being a forest ranger was everything that he thought it would be. Well, almost. Each morning ride through the Rockies was a joy to Ricky. Without doubts the Rocky Mountains were the most beautiful place on God's earth, he had the privilege of patrolling it on horseback. He felt a sense of freedom and peace each day that he looked down into the river valleys and each time he passed between the clusters of tall snow-covered pine trees. The air was cold, crisp, and filled with the sweet aroma of the evergreens. The feeling of the cool winter breeze blowing against his brown police uniform and against his "Smokey the Bear" hat filled him with a sense of pleasure and satisfaction. During his years as an officer, he had made numerous arrests for poaching, possession of illegal substances, theft, graffiti, and public intoxication. His duty to enforce the laws of the U.S. Forest Service gave him a sense of pride and also a deep sense of duty. This northern section of the Rocky Mountains was his backyard, and he was the keeper of it. He loved riding Claire through the magnificent Colorado Rocky Mountain trails. Claire was young, massive, powerful, and she had a trusting bond with him that only Ricky could explain. As he rode along, he often scratched the side of her neck, reassuring her of his fondness for her. The heat rising from Claire's hot back gave him additional warmth in the cold weather. He felt safer on Claire, than he did on foot, because he knew that if he had to move fast, Claire could carry him faster than his own two feet could. Not only was Claire his friend, but she was also his security. Truly she was a magnificent animal! Claire was his first horse and he was her first assigned rider.

Ricky was riding slowly along the winding snow-covered dirt trail known by rangers as the "Northland Trail." This particular trail seldom saw any hikers during December, but had been used in the past by people who committed crimes. The Northland Trail was one of four areas that had the highest occurrences of crimes. The entire area was covered in a thick blanket of fresh snow. As Ricky rode along, the light snow fell quietly and there was almost no breeze. During his ten years as a law enforcement officer, Ricky had never been in a volatile situation that required him to fire his weapon at any living thing. Today, all that was about to change.

The creature was watching him from a distance of perhaps one hundred yards away. Since it was downwind from Ricky, Claire was unable to pick up its scent. The creature quietly stalked the horse and its rider from the top of the mountain ridge. Its last kill was several days ago. It was hungry, really hungry. It made its descent, and it was coming quickly. Being a surprisingly large predator that it was, it stalked its prey as quietly as a mountain lion, which was also part of its diet. The distance between the creature and the unsuspecting ranger closed to perhaps fifty yards as it crept up behind them. The creature was still at a much higher elevation but the distance was steadily decreasing. Ricky and Claire had no idea that the creature there. The creature was well concealed among the tall snow-covered evergreens, pines, and boulders as it got closer and closer.

"Echo 9 . . . Camp 1" came over Ricky's radio.

"Go for Echo 9" replied Ricky.

"What's your 10-20?" asked Camp 1.

"Northland Trail, half a mile south of the Canton River." replied Ricky.

"10-4" replied Camp 1.

Suddenly, and eerie feeling overcame Ricky. Something didn't seem right. What he once described as his "sixth sense" was alerting him to something out the ordinary. Ricky began to feel that someone or something was watching him. He stopped Claire and quickly looked around him and then behind him.

Is something watching me? Was it a mountain lion, a bear, a wolf, a poacher, or something else watching? he thought to himself.

All he could see through the falling snow were, snow covered evergreens, boulders, hills, ridges, and a few dirt paths coming down the side of a ridge. He continued to quickly scan the mountainous terrain around him to see if he could spot any kind of movement. After a minute of fruitless search, he pulled out his service issued binoculars and repeated his scan of the area. Still he could see nothing.

Not a creature or person of any kind could be seen.

But why this weird sensation? There is something is not right, here! he thought.

The wind began to whip up and blow harder into his face. For this reason, Claire did not pick up on the creature's scent, which was behind her. The creature was behind him and above him on the ridge and was still making its slow descent towards the ranger. It was time to eat! Not a single twig broke under the creature's feet and not a single rock shifted or was kicked aside as it slowly and quietly stepped down towards its prey. Tall trees and boulders large enough to hide a truck provided perfect concealment for the massive beast. Suddenly something alarmed Claire, causing her to raise up on her hind legs and neigh loudly. The raising up on her two hind legs nearly threw Ricky off of her back. Ricky gripped the reigns and Claire's mane frantically in an effort to keep from being thrown to the ground. He had never seen Claire become as jittery as this before. He stopped her and began to spin Claire around in slow circle, yet again, to scan the ridge, boulders, and trees.

Was it a bear, a mountain lion, or what?" Ricky thought. As quickly as he could he regain control of the horse, he suddenly he noticed the odor.

What is that rank smell? Ricky thought to himself. The stench reminded him, not of a carcass, but of a large shaggy dog that was never bathed by its owner. The smell was faint at first, but quickly became overpowering.

Was that what a bear is supposed to smell like? he thought. After a couple of minutes, he decided to continue on along the winding trail. He would reach Canton River soon, and be able to stop for cup of coffee at the local diner.

But what about that stink? Where was it coming from? he continued to think.

Ricky was ready for any bear or mountain lion. He had a Remington 870 police shotgun on "hot standby" position. The gun was load with five rounds of one ounce slugs.

Five slugs should bring down a bear! he thought. He also had his service-issued .40 S&W pistol. Claire continued to neigh loudly. For the first time, Ricky could Claire's body tremble. That was very odd! Ricky was really starting to have a difficult time controlling her.

"Claire, Claire" he whispered, while stroking her neck, trying to calm the equine.

Suddenly, out of the corner of his eye, Ricky saw some kind of movement. With lightning speed and perfect accuracy, he whipped the pistol out of his holster, spun his body to the right to 180 degrees and placed his front sight on large grey center mass and pulled the trigger. The round struck the creature in the left side of its torso as it swung its massive shaggy arm in an apparent effort to grab him. Instead of grabbing Ricky, the creature's huge clawed hand slammed against his chest with such force that it sent him flying backwards off of his mount. The clawed hand's impact also knocked the pistol out of Ricky's hand. Ricky sailed through the air backwards and landed onto a patch of snow covered leaves, slightly off of the dirt trail. The pistol landed near his right hand. As he picked up his head and looking past his boots, he saw Claire's head slam against the ground near his boots. Ricky could see that blood was coming out her Claire's nostrils as he lost consciousness.

How long he lay in the snow, he could not tell. He awoke to the feeling of someone's hand squeezing his own.

"Ricky! Ricky!" said the Emergency Medical Technician. Ricky looked around him and saw two medical technicians, Supervisor Ranger Gaines, and Ranger Lyons staring down at him. "Ricky, press your feet against my hands!" said the medic. Ricky gave a good firm push with his feet.

"Good that indicates you've got nerve communication to your legs." said the medic.

The two medical technicians quickly loaded him onto an EMT board, secured his neck, and placed Ricky into a helicopter that was waiting less than only fifty yards away. He lost consciousness again.

Chapter 2

Good Afternoon Ricky

T he first thing that Ricky saw as he awoke was a white vase filled with flowers, sitting in the center of small stained wooden stand in front of him. He discovered himself inclined in bed with an IV tube attached to his arm. Looking around he noticed that the bed beside him was empty. He looked up on the wall and saw that the clock indicated 8:35 a.m. He reached over to pour himself a cup of water, but then quickly ceased the attempt when he noticed a sharp pain in his chest. He looked down to discover that his chest was tightly wrapped in some kind of brace.

What happened to my chest? He thought to himself. He pressed the red button near his bed. Not only was he experiencing pain, but also a great sense of hunger.

"Nurse, can I have breakfast please . . . and coffee too?"

"I'll bring it as soon as I can!" came a nurse's reply. Five minutes later, the nurse brought in a hot breakfast and coffee.

"What happened to my chest?" he asked her.

"You have some broken ribs. Try to take it easy, okay?."
She politely replied. She quickly left the room to resume her
duties.

What? Broken ribs? How? he thought to himself. As he ate,
he tried to think back and figure out why he even here in the
hospital. For a few minutes he wondered if he was in some
kind of car accident, or if he fallen down in the woods. Nothing
came to mind. Suddenly, he stopped eating. Suddenly it
became clearer what had happened to him. Memories and
flashbacks of the encounter with the creature began to fill
his heart and entire being with terror. Suddenly he was lost
in thought as he recalled seeing the shaggy, dirty-looking,
creature standing above Claire. Being mounted as high as
he was, he remembered actually looked into the creatures
large, ash grey colored, shaggy face. He remembered seeing
the massive head, huge jaw and four fangs. The head was
surrounded by appeared to be a shaggy mane. He then
recalled how the creature gave out a nightmarish roar, as if
it was roaring at its worst enemy. The memory of the loud
hideous roar sent a jolt of fear through his body, causing a
sharp pain in his chest. He dropped his fork onto the plate as
he placed his hand over his chest. He gave out a shriek as
another wave of pain pulsed throughout his chest. He began
to cough uncontrollably causing the agony of his injuries to
intensify. Things were getting worse with each cough! The pain
caused him to knock the breakfast tray to floor. He frantically
reached for the button to summon the nurse. "Aaaack!" he
shrieked into speaker phone. Within a minute the nurse came
running in to help him. She gave him a painkiller and ordered
him to lay still and close his eyes.

As he lay still with his eyes closed he thought to himself:
*Whose gonna believe that I saw such a creature? People
are gonna think that I am another prankster or disillusioned
person! What makes matters worse is that I wear a law
enforcement uniform! How are other rangers and other cops
going to look at me now? How in the world am I gonna put*

this in my official report? These thoughts, and many others, played and replayed in his mind as the pain killer began to take effect. Before he knew it, he was sound asleep.

At 12:00 p.m. grey-haired Supervisory Ranger Rusty Gaines stuck his head in the door and gave a big, cheesy, mustached smile."Good afternoon Ricky!" smiled Rusty.

"Good afternoon!" smiled Ricky.

"How do you feel Ricky?" asked Rusty.

"Chest hurts. Other than that, okay, I guess" said Ricky.

"You look like you had a rough morning! Whatsa' matter, the poachers too much for ya?" joked Rusty.

"Yeah, they were!" Ricky laughed.

Rusty helped himself to Ricky's pot of coffee, sat on the empty bed next to Ricky, and folded hands.

"Congratulations Ricky, you've got three broken ribs!" smiled Rusty.

"Oh, so that's why I've been hurting! Well, at least I'm alive." Rickey smiled.

"Yeah, Thank God for that! It's also good to see that your spirits are up!" said Rusty.

The red alarm on your radio sounded off. When you didn't answer, we sent a helicopter to your last 10-20. We spotted you just off of the path next to a very large pool of blood. Evidently, it was Claire's blood and not yours! It looks as though Claire was dragged up the ridge. After about an hour of searching for Claire, we called it off, because the snow storm. I've never known of any bear that could drag off something as big as a horse!" said Rusty.

"Really?" asked Ricky, pretending to go along with what he just heard.

Ricky looked at the vase in front of him and wondered. *Hmmm, I'd better be real careful in what I say. Would this guy really believe me, if I tell him everything?* Ricky thought to himself.

After a minute of awkward silence, Ricky decided to take a gamble.

"It wasn't a bear, Mr. Rusty." said Ricky.

Rusty's salt and pepper eyebrows lifted in obvious surprise, or perhaps disbelief.

Oh boy, here it comes! I really messed up now! Ricky thought.

"What?" Rusty calmly asked.

After a few seconds, Ricky mumbled, "It roared at me."

"It roared at you? Well, what did it sound like?" asked Rusty.

"It sounded different. It sounded like an angry roar, or a wail. Very loud!" Ricky said.

"What was it?" asked Rusty.

I don't know what it was." replied Ricky.

"What do you mean you don't know what it was? Can you describe it?" asked Rusty.

"Bigger than me . . . hairy . . . kind of an ash gray in color. It had big teeth."

"Really? Now this is getting interesting!" laughed Rusty.

"I think I shot it . . . yeah I shot it." said Ricky.

"You shot it? Oh this is getting better by the minute!" laughed Rusty.

"Your sidearm was only about a foot away from your hand. An inspection of it did show that it was discharged.

Amazingly, we found the empty casing nearby, too." said Rusty.

"Ricky, your jacket and bullet proof vest were shredded. How did that happen?" asked Rusty.

"It reached for me, or swung at me, or something like that. That's all I remember." said Ricky.

Rusty looked at Ricky inquisitively for a few a moments and then looked around the room. Ricky could see in Rusty's expression that Rusty was deep in thought.

"So . . . what was it Ricky?"

"Well . . . it stood on two legs."

"What?" asked Rusty with a surprised look on his face.

"Big, shaggy, ash gray. Irises as black as coal. It was so loud! It smelled bad . . . really bad!" said Ricky.

Rusty looked at Ricky for another minute, without saying a word. This made Ricky feel very uncomfortable.

What does he think of me? Ricky thought to himself.

Finally, Rusty broke the silence.

"Ricky, are you telling me you saw a Sasquatch or something like that?

"I saw what I described to you." replied Ricky carefully. Ricky looked again at the vase in front of him now wishing he didn't say so much about the incident.

"You don't believe me don't you? I can tell by that look on your face." said Ricky.

Rusty looked at him for a few seconds, turned and walked to the window and looked out.

Oh great! This is not looking good for me! thought Ricky.

Rusty walked back, looking down at the floor, but obviously grinning.

After an brief moment of silence Rusty looked up and began to speak.

"Well hold on now. Maybe I do believe you . . . . we found those unusually large clawed footprints next to the pool of blood. We photographed them and followed them and the trail of blood up a one thousand feet ridge, but we had to stop the pursuit due to the snowstorm." Rusty smiled and widened his eyes in an effort to emphasize what he just revealed. Ricky's eyes widened at what Rusty said.

He actually believes me! Ricky thought within himself.

"Are you serious! You actually have photographs of footprints, Mr. Gaines?"

"You bet we did!" laughed Rusty."Ricky, for the longest time I thought those monster stories was garbage, but seeing that long trail of blood and large footprints has really got me curious of the matter. We're still investigating it. We want to find out for ourselves what could drag off an animal as big as a horse up the side of a mountain. Ricky, you may be released from the hospital in a few more days. I scheduled you for a couple of months of medical leave. Start writing your preliminary report on this incident at home as soon as possible. Wait about 72 hours, so that you can get your thoughts together." said Rusty.

"10-4" said Ricky.

"Well . . . I'm headed back to the station. I couldn't stay for long. I'll talk to you soon. Bye!"

Leaving so soon?" asked Ricky.

"You bet . . . busy man! Take it real easy, Ricky!"

"Mr. Gaines can you bring me my personal laptop from my office? With it, I can start my narrative of the event. I want to start on today. The laptop is sitting next to my desktop computer."

"Sure, I'll fetch it for ya', but you'll have to wait until tomorrow."

"A station handheld radio, too? I want to monitor radio traffic. Maybe another ranger will see the creature or maybe some hikers may tell us of it." asked Ricky.

"Yeah, I think I can do that." replied Rusty.

"Gotta' run!" said Rusty.

"Have a good day, Sir!" replied Ricky.

Gaines left the room. Ricky began to think deeply on the incident. The idea that this was the closest he ever came to losing his life struck him with awe. Emotions of awe, terror, and confusion began to fill his mind as he thought about the creature's hideous face and cavernous mouth.

Those creatures are actually real! Why didn't the creature kill me? Did it prefer horse meat over human meat or what? He thought to himself. Distinct images of the creature replayed through his mind over and over again. The beast was big, very big and taller than any man he had ever known. He was mounted on a large horse, but still found himself looking into its eyes! The creature had broad shoulders, long, shaggy, ash grey colored hair. Ricky didn't notice any whites in its eyes, but complete blackness. Its face looked vaguely like a gorilla, but it wasn't a gorilla. It was distinctly different. As far as he knew, he was the first person to ever be assaulted by such a creature. Ricky's mind then went to his horse. Poor Claire! How disgusting and ghastly that his partner was killed and probably eaten. Ricky started the mounted patrol detail five years ago. Claire was his first and only horse he ever had. She was such a fine service horse! The Service would give him another horse, but it wouldn't be the same. How sad it would be without Claire! Thoughts bombarded his mind. He was angry that the creature took his beloved horse. Yet again, could he really blame the creature? It is a predator, and what do predators do? They hunt, not because they are evil and bloodthirsty, but because they are hungry and need food to survive.

I'll have to chalk this one up as a bad encounter with a hungry wild animal! he thought to himself.

"Nurse!" called Ricky over the hospital pager. The nurse arrived.

"Can I please have a sharp pencil, clipboard, and maybe five sheets of printer paper?"

"Uh . . . yeah, sure!" replied the nurse.

After about ten minutes, the nurse returned. Ricky waited for the nurse to leave before he began sketching pictures of the beast which he would incorporate into his official report. A few minutes later he heard the sound of her footsteps coming towards his room. He quickly turned the pages over so that she, or whoever it was, would not be able to see what he was drawing. The sound of the footsteps was just another nurse that was passing by. Ricky resumed his drawings. After about thirty minutes, he was done. He looked at all five pages and chuckled. He felt like a third grader in school drawing pictures of his favorite monster.

Chapter 3

Paleontologist

On the second day that Ricky Toomis was in the hospital, Ranger Rusty Gaines returned with Ricky's laptop. Gaines walked in to find Ricky sipping coffee as he was sitting up in the hospital bed.

"Well, well, how is Ricky boy?" said Rusty, in a jolly manner.

"Here's your laptop and a service radio!"

"My laptop! Now you're talking!" replied Ricky.

Ricky was was eager to have the laptop so that he could carefully build his narrative regarding the attack.

"Hey . . . thanks Mr. Gaines!" smiled Ricky.

"Ricky, when are you leaving the hospital?"

"The doctor told me, I can in few more days."

"Well that's good. You've got a couple of months off of work. If you need more, which I think you might, just call me, and I'll take care of it for you." said Rusty.

"I appreciate it!" replied it Ricky.

"Has there been any news from the other rangers about that thing that attacked me?"

"No, nothing at all. No one has seen or heard anything. "Was the media there?" asked Ricky.

"Yes, but we told them that you were attacked by a bear. The media still reported it as a possible bear attack or monster attack. Unfortunately, the media was also able to photograph the large footprints, before we forced them out of the area. Hopefully news flash will be soon forgotten." said Rusty. "Has the Service put out a public safety announcement yet?" asked Ricky.

"No we haven't, and I'll explain why. If we put out information on it too soon, it will be your word versus the words of the public. The majority of the word is still skeptical about the existences of this thing. We don't want to put out any 'monster stories' yet, until we have more evidence, like a monster's body, or anything that would be undeniable. Until then, it is best that we keep silent towards the media. We're going to try to keep this matter 'in house' for the time being." "And if it kills a person?" asked Ricky.

"If it kills a person, which hopefully it doesn't, then we will make a public safety announcement. I can only image what will happen once we go to the media with this."

"Mr. Gaines, all my life I never believed the stories about some hairy monster running loose in the woods. That was no man in some silly suit that attacked me, it wasn't even human, it wasn't a gorilla, it was just . . . . bizarre! It will take down a horse, what is to stop it from taking something smaller, like a person?" said Ricky.

"That is good question, Ricky. There is a potential that it could take a human, if it wanted to." agreed Rusty.

"One the flip side, if that thing is really what you described it to be, we've got a really big discovery on our hands! This is going to be the story of the century!" laughed Gaines, shaking his head from side to side.

"I'm glad you actually believe me, and not think that I am some kind of nut or something!" said Ricky.

"To be honest, if it wasn't for those huge footprints and that massive pool of blood at the incident scene, I definitely would have thought you were crazy!" laughed Gaines.

"Well, I've got to go back to the field. Start your narrative on the incident. Take it easy, get some rest, and don't flirt too much with those pretty nurses! Leave that up to me!" laughed Rusty.

"You'll win them with that gray mustache of yours!" laughed Ricky.

"That's right!" winked Rusty as he left the room.

Ricky turned on the police radio and his laptop. He began typing his narrative describing his encounter with the massive creature on that snowy trail. His narrative included every material detail that he could remember, even the memory of the odor that he noticed, just minutes before the attack that killed Claire and nearly claimed his own life. After thirty minutes of writing, his narrative was complete. He saved a copy of the narrative onto his a flash drive, and planned to bring it to his office to be copied to the agency's law enforcement case program. Ricky spent the next day just resting, watching the news, monitoring his police radio, and hoping to hear if any other rangers had encounters with the monster. He also hoped that some ranger would be notified by hikers of any encounters with the strange beast. To his disappointment, he didn't hear anything over the radio communications, other than common, everyday ranger transmissions; an arrest incident regarding a poacher, and a rescue of a motorist who was stranded on a snowy road. A week after the encounter with the creature, Ricky arrived at the office in blue jeans, plaid shirt, and a bright yellow, hooded coat. He immediately inserted the flash drive into his computer and within an hour, had an official incident report to give to Rusty Gaines.

"Mr. Gaines, here's the report of the incident."

"Just place it in my inbox; I'll be able to get to it as soon as I can." replied Gaines, as he continued to type on his own computer without looking up.

"Ricky, how's the ribs?" asked Rusty Gaines.

"Still hurts, but he pain killers are doing an okay job of minimizing the pain. I'm going back home to get some rest." said Ricky.

"Okay, I'll get back with you as soon as I get the rest of this stuff done." said Gains as he continued typing and filing papers.

"Officer Toomis, there's a man here to see you. His name is Dr. Leo Kluud, a paleontologist from the University of Colorado" said Anne, the records technician.

"But I am off-duty, Anne . . . aawwhh . . . send him on in!" sighed Ricky.

"I can tell him that you already went home." said Anne.

"No, just send him on it. Did he give you the reason for his visit?" asked Ricky.

"He said he wanted to discuss the incident you were involved with, just last week." said Anne.

Ricky and Rusty looked at each other in stark surprise.

How did a university professor catch wind of the incident regarding the attack? Ricky thought to himself.

"Officer Toomis, I'm Dr. Leo Kluud, Professor of Palentology from the University of Colorado." said Dr. Kluud, handing Ricky his university identification card. Dr. Kluud appeared to be about sixty years old, had a long white bear, white hair with a few remaining black strands, and a big round nose. He was wearing round, "John Lennon style" wire-rimmed thick glasses and out-of-style brown sports coat with elbow patches. His necktie was incorrectly tied, old and also out of style. He wore a brown "old man's hat." He wore decent black slacks, and decent brown loafers. He carried an old-looking leather briefcase with buckles. In every way, he fit the package of being some kind of college professor, someone's grandpa, and Santa Claus without a red suit.

"I'm Ranger Ricky Toomis. I'm pleased to meet you Dr. Kluud." greeted Ricky.

"Please, just call me Leo." said the professor, cordially.

"Okay, Leo. How can I help you?" asked Ricky.

"Officer Toomis, Last week I saw the brief news flash regarding the encounter you had a bear. I wanted to take just a little of your time, if it would be okay with you." said the professor in a polite but urgent manner.

News flash? Oh no! Ricky thought to himself.

"Come in, sit down. Can I offer you some coffee?" asked Ricky respectfully.

"Yes, thank you!" replied Leo, rather surprised at the respect given him by the officer. "Officer Toomis, how long have you been a Ranger?" asked Leo.

"Ten years." replied Ricky.

"Wow, that's impressive! Are you married?" asked Leo.

"No, I haven't found the right person yet." replied Ricky.

"How about you, Leo, are you married?" asked Ricky.

"Yes, sir! I also have two sons and six grandchildren." replied Dr. Kludd proudly.

"You must be a proud grandfather!" said Ricky smiling. "Indeed I am!" replied Leo smiling.

So this is what Santa Claus sounds like! Ricky laughed within himself.

Leo looked at Ricky and smiled. "You look well! How do you feel, Officer Toomis?"

"Okay." replied Ricky

"Just call me Ricky." said Ricky.

"Very well, Ricky." said Leo.

"How can I help you today, Leo?" asked Ricky, respectfully.

"As I mentioned, it came to my attention that you were attacked by a bear." replied Leo. "When the rescue helicopter was dispatched to find you, the media rushed in also. The media photographed the pool of blood and the bloody trail that went up to the top of the ridge. They reported you were attacked by a bear. I wanted to ask you if it was a bear, or something else." said Leo.

Ricky, tried to maintain a "poker face" as he looked at Leo. After a brief moment he answered.

"Leo, I really appreciate the time you took to come here today, but I am very busy and I have to go . . ."

"Ricky, I was able to obtain a copy of the photos of the footprints where you were attacked. It wasn't a bear wasn't it?" Leo bluntly asked.

"I have no comment." said Ricky. Ricky paused and sat silent, looking away from Leo.

"I didn't think so, since bears don't walk up mountain ridges on two legs. I also didn't think that a bear could drag a full-grown horse up to the top of such a steep ridge. It didn't sound like something that a bear would normally do. I began to ponder what kind of an animal would do that. I thought and thought for a while on the information that I had received and I couldn't come up with any animal that could do that. To tell you the truth, I was rather puzzled. I have idea of what might have attacked you, but I thought that I it would be a good idea to come and get more information from you about this." said Leo. Ricky and Mr. Gaines exchanged quick glances at each other. Ricky began to wonder how much he should tell the professor. "Ricky, I am a professor of paleontology, not a reporter for some tabloid. You've seen my credentials. I am not here to get a fantastic story or make you look like a fool. I don't even plan of going to me media. I am here because I might be able to provide you information which may help you in your investigation. I am just asking for your cooperation." said Leo frankly.

"Go ahead, Ricky. You've got my permission." interjected Rusty.

"Ricky, were you or anyone able to photograph the animal?" Leo went on.

"No . . . but I did make some sketches of the creature." said Ricky.

"Sketches? May I see please them?" asked Leo.

Ricky handed a manila folder to Leo. Leo examined all ten sketches intently for nearly five minutes. Ricky and Rusty, sat there and looked at the Leo as he furrowed his brow over the sketches. Afterwards, Leo asked, "Can I make copies these?" "Sure, only if you promise me that you don't share them with the media or anyone." said Ricky.

"You have my promise." assured Leo.

"The copier is right behind you." replied Ricky.

"Thank you. Just give me a quick minute." said Leo.

While the professor walked over to the copier, Ricky and Rusty began to talk.

"Well, he is a professor. This may prove very useful." said Rusty.

"Maybe so!" replied Ricky.

A couple of minutes later the professor came back and handed the original sketches to Ricky.

"Thank you again, Ricky" said Leo.

"You're very welcome, Leo." replied Ricky."Ricky the pictures you sketch are the similar to what I expected. I have been studying this cryptoid for maybe twenty years now. Your incident was very exciting to me so I made it a point to see you as soon as you very well enough to come back to your office. Also, the fact that you lost a government service horse gives me more reason to believe that you really did encounter something out of the ordinary."

"I see." said Ricky.

"Ricky, there have been numerous hoaxes regarding this creature for centuries. For longest time I considered the stories as hoaxes or something that could be easily explained. You, being a federal law enforcement officer, would naturally make me inclined to believe the veracity of your statements regarding such a sighting as this. The sketches you made resemble a creature once known as 'Gigantopithecus blacki.'" "I'm sorry, but what did you call it?" asked Ricky. "'Gigantopithecus blacki. It means, 'Black's Giant Ape. This animal was believed to be an extinct ape from Southeast Asia, standing perhaps almost 10 feet tall and weighing perhaps 1,200 lbs. We have three fossilized skeletons and more than a thousand teeth of what we believe came from the 'Gigantopithecus blacki.' The positioning of its skull, neck bone, and jaw structure suggests that the creature walked on two legs." said Leo.

"I didn't notice how it walked; I just discovered it standing on two legs behind me." said Ricky.

"Did you see its face?" Leo asked.

"Yes, it vaguely resembled an ape or a really angry one." he replied, lifting his eyebrows.

"Vaguely? I see." said Leo, with obvious curiosity.

"Ricky, I want to ask you. What do you or other rangers intend to do, if you encounter this creature again?" asked Leo. "If it poses another threat to me or anyone, I'll shoot to stop it." replied Ricky.

"And if it doesn't pose a threat?" asked Leo.

"We were instructed to follow it from a distance." Ricky replied. "I see." smiled Leo.

"Ricky, I want to go out with you to study the animal." said Leo.

"Well, that will be fine, but you have to wait for a couple of months." Rusty interjected.

"Why, if I may ask?" asked Leo.

"The creature broke three of my ribs." said Ricky.

"What? How did it do that." asked Leo with obvious surprise." "I am not sure. I think it swung at me or something. The next thing I knew, I was in the hospital. I'll get back to you in a couple of months." replied Ricky.

"Very well." said Leo.

"It sure took a long time for it to come out of hiding! There haven't been any real eye-witness reports of it for a while." said Ricky.

"I definitely haven't heard of any reports of it for years." agreed Leo.

"Ricky, would it be okay with you if I make a suggestion?" asked Leo.

Oh boy, here it comes! thought Ricky.

"Sure, Leo, what is your suggestion?" asked Ricky.

"Ricky, do not kill the animal, but trap it or perhaps tranquilize it for me."

I knew you were going to say that! Ricky thought.

"Leo, that thing nearly killed me . . ." Ricky protested."But it didn't. It took your horse, not you. Think about this for a minute, a horse can kill you with one kick or even bite off a man's entire hand. A horse can do more damage with its natural weapons than an unarmed man. The creature that attacked you went for the bigger and more powerful animal. Why did it do that?"

Hmmm, that's a good question! Ricky thought within himself. "I don't know." replied Ricky after a few seconds.

"I suppose that you weren't its first choice of food. The horse, obviously was." explained Leo.

"You want us to take this creature alive?" asked Rusty.

"Yes." replied the professor.

Both Ricky and Rusty looked at each other.

"A dosage potent enough for large gorilla might be sufficient to put it out for a little while." replied Leo.

"Well, it was a lot bigger than a gorilla. How about a dosage strong enough for an elephant?" asked Ricky while shaking his head.

"Perhaps! Whatever you think it would take!" laughed Leo. "Ricky, this creature may be the last of its kind. If so, it would be a great loss to the scientific community and to the world if it goes into extinction like so many other species already have." said Leo.

"Well I agree, but, but if it does kill a person, something has got to be done about it." said Rusty.

"Maybe it not the last of its kind." suggested Ricky.

"I hope you are correct about that." replied Leo.

"Would you please consider having it captured alive, Ricky?"
"Yes, I'll consider it, Leo, but, like I said, if it poses a threat to anyone else, it may be shot in order to protect others." said Ricky.

The professor looked at the picture taken just a few months earlier, of the Ricky mounted on his horse."

"Ricky, I am sorry about the loss of your horse. I understand that officers are usually attached to their horses or their canines." said Leo.

"You are right on that, Leo." said Ricky, looking at a picture on the wall of him atop of Claire. Ricky's sadness in losing Claire started to grow.

"Please remember what I have said. You can see I am deeply interested in this creature. I really want to be able to have one captured and protected. I'll do more research on this creature this week, and forward all of my findings to your office. The information I provide you may be useful." said Leo.

"I agree." said Ricky.

"Please consider my request." said Leo.

"I'll keep everything you've said in mind." replied Ricky.

"Ricky, here's my business card. Please give me a call anytime, or email me. Get plenty of rest. The sooner you are fully healed the better for you and the better for everyone. Gentlemen, I won't take any more of your time. I do want to thank you sincerely for allowing me to visit your office today." smiled Leo.

"It was a pleasure meeting you, Leo." said Ricky.

As Leo walked toward the door, he turned and looked at Ricky.

"Ricky, I hope to hear from you soon." said Leo.

"Okay!" said Ricky.

"I'll be going now. Again, you get lots of rest, okay?" asked

Leo politely smiling.

"You bet I will!" replied Ricky, returning the smile.

Leo left the office and walked down the sidewalk.

"Ricky, what did he have to say?" asked Anne.

"Well . . . not a lot." replied Ricky.

Chapter 4

Bernie Lukey

Bernie Lukey, former defensive end with Colorado State University, was a profane, hot-headed, six feet four inches tall red head man and weighing in at two hundred and seventy five pounds. His passions in life were football, bow hunting, and body-building. He graduated from Colorado State University just a year earlier with a degree in Physical Education. He attended the university on a full four-year football scholarship. At the age of fifteen, he killed his first twelve-point buck with his father's compound bow. He cherished that mounted kill as much as he did his football trophies. Today he was hoping to bring home another buck, although a doe would be fine too. He had been longing for some good venison for several weeks now and he was feeling lucky today. He was sure that he would come home with something, after several dry weeks of not even seeing anything at all.

Bernie sat halfway up a ridge and hidden behind some large white rocks. It was a favorite hiding spot he had found many years earlier while scouting around ridges for well concealed shooting spots. He liked coming up to this rocky outcrop. The trek upward through the ridges offered him a superb workout. By the time he reached the large rocks, his legs were burning, his chest was pounding, and he found himself gasping for air. This was the perfect shooting position! From this vantage point, Bernie always felt like he completely owned the valley in front of him. He had a superb view of the ridges both to his left and to his right. From his vantage point, he would be well-concealed and yet still able to easily fire his compound bow in any direction. The ridges were full of snow-covered ponderosa pines and bunched grass. As he made himself comfortable, he pulled out his binoculars and began to view the surrounding snowy ridges. As he waited he nibbled on some jerky and drank Gatorade. After nearly an hour of periodic peering through his binoculars, he finally spotted what he was looking for. *Ah ha!* He thought. As he peered down the ridge towards the creek, he a spotted a lone, solitary buck coming out from a dense patched of snow covered pines. It was amazing close, perhaps only seventy five meters down the ridge. Only the head and neck was visible. The rest of the body was behind a tree. The buck stood motionless for several minutes. After a while, it slowly stepped out. Bernie was then able to see its entire body. It was a huge, healthy, and possibly a twelve point buck! Since the wind was blowing into Bernie's face, the buck didn't pick up on his scent. *Oooh! This is a big one . . . at least 175 pounds!* he thought to himself. The animal slowing walked along, completely oblivious to the hunter that was crouched far above it. The buck walking slowly through the snow, grabbing an occasional stalk of grass as it approached a larger grassy knoll. Bernie very slowly and carefully put down the binoculars, slowly reached for his compound bow and slowly pulled the arrow out of his quiver. He slowly and silently placed the arrow on the bowstring, smoothly pulled the string back and took aim. He waited. The buck lowered its head, grabbed a large mouthful of grass, and lifted its head. It stood there and chewed, not having a care in the world, and not knowing that Bernie's arrow was sighted on its head. Between this third and fourth breath, he released the bowstring. *Thwock!* The arrow flew and penetrated deep within the neck of the unsuspecting buck. It dropped hard, like a rock, kicking its legs for a couple of minutes and then it lay completely still. "Whooooohooooo!" he laughed aloud. Waves of excitement, like electricity from his head to his toes, ran through his body.

Bernie was unaware that at this moment, he was both the hunter and the hunted, for far behind him, the creature was watching Bernie from an even higher vantage point. Tucked in tightly among huge boulders, the creature peered around the huge boulders to look at the two-legged prey, just below it. After silently watching Bernie for nearly fifteen minutes, the shaggy monster began to stalk its way slowly and silently down the ridge towards the unsuspecting human. The wind that blew into Bernie's face suddenly stopped and air was completely still. Bernie thought it rather strange that the wind would stop so abruptly. Not knowing why, Bernie began to feel an inexplicable eeriness as if something was terribly wrong!

Bernie suddenly noticed a strong stink in the air that apparently came out of nowhere!

What on earth is that smell? he thought. He looked around and could see nothing but the white snowy ridges, giant boulders, and snow-covered trees. Trying to ignore the stench, Bernie bent over to secure his bow, quiver, and back-pack. He stood up and secured the fasteners on his backpack when suddenly he heard a cracking sound coming from above him. The sound was that of dry twigs breaking. At first he ignored it. As he looked around him to ensure that he had secured all of his belongings, he heard the cracking of twigs again, only this time, much louder. He decided it was worth a look. Bernie lifted up his eyes to see what was causing the noise. To his horror, he met the eyes of a massive shaggy creature, only about fifty yards away!

What is . . . ? No, that can't be real! He thought. Bernie was shocked to discover that he was not alone, and that an unbelievably large shaggy creature with big teeth and claws was making its way directly towards him. Whatever it was, he could tell it was something he had never encountered

44

before It didn't look very gentle. The hairs on Bernie's neck and arms suddenly stood on end as his eyes took in the new information. Suddenly, it seemed as if Bernie's own sensory organs of sight and hearing became heightened. His eyes and his ears zoomed in onto the oncoming creature. He could actually see the darks eyes of the creature. Bernie wanted to run, his brain screamed out to run, but oddly his legs felt as if they were cemented into the snow! *I've got to run! I've got to run!* Bernie thought to himself. Bernie started to quake with an uncontrollable fear. Its massive shaggy legs walked sure-footedly down the steep pathless ridge. The sound of breaking twigs and sticks grew louder and louder. He looked into the face of the monster and saw its large black eyes. He could even see the canine fangs extended from both the upper and lower jaw. He also knew it definitely wasn't a bear, because bears don't walk down ridges on two legs. It wasn't human either; it appeared to be a lot bigger and taller than he was! It was nearly four times wider than Bernie's own muscular frame. A slight wind resumed and whipped against the creature's long shaggy coat. It continued to walk down towards him in a stiff, weird gate. Bernie could now make out its' long clawed hands on its stiffly swinging arms. The claws were black and sinister looking, very predatory in appearance. The feet had unusually long clawed toes and continued to make a strange clicking sound as the nails made contact with any large rock that it stepped onto. Bernie couldn't help but try to stare into the creature's shaggy looking face which he unable to identify as anything he had ever saw before. The creature's face slightly resembled an angry gorilla, but then again, it maybe not, for it was weirdly different! The eyes were large and black as coal, and they didn't appear to have any color other than black. The creature then jutted it head towards and reached out towards Bernie, while opening its clawed hands and let out a loud angry roar. The roar was loud enough to announce its presence to the entire world! It showed all of its teeth as it began to snarl like a threatening wolf. All this Bernie took in at a moment's notice. Suddenly, the creature began to walk downwards towards Bernie at a quicker and more determined pace. Upon seeing the creature speed up, Bernie decided he had better get mobile himself, in the opposite direction! The sound of the breaking twigs sounded deafening to his frozen ears was more than he could handle. Then, somehow, he broke free from the mind-gripping terror he was held by, and immediately he was able to quickly threw down his heavy, overloaded back pack, turn away, and run along a path on the ridge. He still maintained his grip on the bow. The quiver slapped against his back as he ran through the snowy pathless ridge, jumping over rocks and dodging trees. He ran about twenty yards along the only path that went laterally across the ridge. When he looked behind him to see what had become of the creature, he saw it leaping over his backpack at an incredible speed. Bernie turned again and continued running, faster now. After about thirty seconds Bernie came to a rock waterfall that he would have to carefully climb down to a large flat cap rock fifteen feet below him. As Bernie descended downwards to the cap rock, the creature had veered off its pursuit and scrambled down a different path! *What?!* thought Bernie as he saw the creature took a slightly different path that Bernie had somehow missed. As Bernie grabbed hold onto the snowy rocks and tree roots and scrambled down onto the cap rock, he looked over and realized the creature had headed him off and now stood but twenty yards in front of him. As it made its way forward, the creature began to raise both of its arms and reached out towards him, roared again. It slowly began advancing on Bernie as he looked for another way off the ledge. Bernie looked back again at the clawed arms that were getting closer to him. He instinctively backed up and immediately felt his back hit the steep rock waterfall. Frantically he looked around again for a place to run but found that he had blocked himself in. Bernie was surrounded by large boulders and trees on each side of him! There was nowhere to run but forward where the creature was standing! He was sure he could not climb back up the rock waterfall fast enough to get away. With a conviction that surprised even himself, he yelled; "*Not without a fight buddy!*" With that, he reached over his shoulder, pulled out a razor-tipped arrow, set it on the bowstring, and as fast as he could, took aim at the creature's chest. The creature seemed oblivious to what Bernie was about to do and continued its slow advance. Once his aim was sure, Bernie let the arrow fly. *Thwock!* The arrow sunk deep into the chest of the creature, causing it to let out a deafening high-pitched wail. It grabbed at the arrow and frantically tried to pull it out, roaring or wailing with each pull against the arrow. Bernie quickly reached for another arrow and took aim. He let the arrow fly. *Thwock!* The creature shifted left and right, in an effort to pull out the first arrow. The second arrow flew past the creature and landed into the truck of pine tree. Bernie pulled out a third arrow from his quiver, aimed for the chest again, and let the third arrow fly. *Thwock!* The arrow sunk deep into the shoulder of the beast. The creature let out another high-pitched wail. The wails echoed throughout the canyon. The creature frantically tried to pull out both arrows, but couldn't because of the pain it was inflicting on itself. Suddenly the creature stopped trying to pull the arrows out, and instead advanced towards Bernie. By this time Bernie had the forth arrow already loaded onto the bow. The creature opened its cavernous fanged mouth and let out a loud eerie roar. As it mouth was wide open, Bernie released the arrow. *Thwock!* This arrow, as intend entered the creature's mouth and partially came out of the back its head as the creature roared at Bernie. It suddenly stopped roaring, and with an eerie slowness, the creature fell silently face-first onto the rocks and snow, like a massive tree that had been cut down. The shaggy creature slammed onto the snow, just a few steps away from Bernie's feet. As he breathed heavily, Bernie's knees began to buckle and he before he knew it he fell knee-first into the snow. His body was shaking violently with fear as he looked at the bleeding mass lying in the snow in front of him. After about five minutes, his shaking subsided and he regained his breathing returned to normal. He was able to pull out his cell phone from his jacket pocket and dial 911. "911, What is your emergency?" came a lady's voice over the phone.

"I need help! Please someone help me!" he stammered.

"What is happening sir?"

"I am in Cusher Valley just north of Elk Mountain at the rock waterfall and the old windmill, about one mile south of HWY 8!

I really need help now!"

Bernie thought for a moment and screamed. "I think I'm going to freeze to death, can you help me or not?!"

"Yes Sir! The Ranger Station is not far from you actually. I'll contact the Ranger on duty there. We'll send out a helicopter for you. Please try get out into the open and keep moving around."

Within twenty minutes a rescue helicopter flew overhead. The pilot spotted Bernie's waving his arms. Upon landing onto a large, wide, flat rock shelf, only twenty meters down from Bernie's location, Ranger Toomis and two EMTs hurriedly leaped out. Ranger Toomis began running towards where Bernie was standing. The two EMTs began busying themselves with grabbing first aid equipment and a stretcher. "It's over there! I think it's dead!" said Bernie pointing in the direction of the creature.

"Are you hurt?" Ranger Toomis called out as he approached Bernie.

"No!" replied Bernie. "Look at that over there!"

Ranger Toomis turned in the direction of where Bernie was frantically pointing.

When he looked, he felt his knees starting to buckle as he saw the huge mass lying in the snow. Bernie and Toomis walked carefully towards the shaggy mass lying twenty feet away, fearful that it might suddenly come back to life and grab them. Once they were within a few steps of the creature, they both stopped and just stared at the mass of hair and blood lying in the snow. The EMTs stood beside the Ricky and just stared in disbelief. Toomis pulled out his cell phone and called the desk officer at the ranger station.

"Jones, this is Toomis!" said Ricky.

"Go ahead, Sir!" replied Jones.

"Have you been monitoring the radio?"

"Yes, Mr. Toomis!"

"Jones, Code 77, understood?"

"Code 77, yes, sir!" replied Jones.

Code 77 is the code to communicate information via cell phones. It was an unofficial code used by forest rangers when they didn't want supervisors or the news media from knowing what was going on during "unimportant" field operations.

"Also, have Ranger Laski and Ranger Iksal call me immediately." Ricky added.

"Yes, sir!" came the reply.

"I'll update you shortly, Bye!" Toomis hung up.

"Medic! Do you have a tape measure?"

"Sure do!" replied the medic, handing it to Ricky.

"Please hold this end!" Ricky then extended the tape. The beast was nearly nine feet seven inches long!

"Incredible!" remarked Ricky.

"Whew! I think I put an end to your monster, Ranger!" exclaimed Bernie. Bernie felt a sense of pride, in having to bring down such a big animal. Bernie quickly realized something was wrong when he looked into Ricky's eyes.

"What is it, Ranger?" Bernie asked.

Ricky continued looking at the creature and then gravely replied, "Actually, no. The creature I encountered was ash gray. This one is as black as midnight."

Chapter 5

The University

Within an hour, more than a dozen U.S. Forest Service Rangers were on scene where the dead creature lay.

"Well, it's not like we have a dead mountain lion or bear here! We need to notify some researcher, zoologist, scientists . . . whomever! The first thing that comes to mind is for us contact the University of Colorado at Denver. I am sure their science professors would want to be the first ones to get their hands on this thing so they can identify it!" said Supervisory Ranger Rusty Gaines.

"Sounds like a good start to me, Sir! I'll have the desk officer call the university's science department requesting them to call me!" agreed Ranger Jones.

"Yes, do that!" agreed Gaines.

Within thirty minutes Ranger Jones cell phone rang.

"This is Jones." he answered

"Mr. Jones, this is Dr. Leo Kluud, Professor of Paleontology, of the University of Denver. I was told to call you."

"Professor, are you busy, right now?" asked Ranger Jones.

"I'll be teaching class within a few minutes! Why do you ask?" asked Dr. Kluud.

"Professor, I know this will sound abrupt, but can one of our officers pick you up within the next half-hour?" asked Jones.

"Pick me up? Why?" asked the professor.

"Sir, please keep this between you and I, but we have a specimen that we want you to look at." replied Jones. "Specimen of what? Is it the creature that attacked Ranger Toomis?" asked Dr. Kluud.

"Sir . . . I think it would be best if you could just come out here and see for yourself. Can one of our men come pick you up at your office?"

"Okay, I'll come." replied Dr. Kluud.

"Thank you, our ranger will arrive within half an hour. Bye!" said Jones.

"Bye!" replied the Dr. Kluud.

Dr. Kluud quickly telephoned an associate to teach for him for the next hour, grabbed his coat, hat, camera, voice recorder, and bag of other examination tools. As mentioned, a plain-clothed ranger arrived at the university in his privately owned vehicle, in order to avoid attention. An hour later, the ranger and Dr. Kluud arrived at the incident scene where he noticed a dozen rangers, bearing shotguns, standing in a loose circle. Dr. Kluud climbed up the trail and came up the massive black mass, lying in the snow.

"Oh my!" gasped Dr. Kluud. For nearly a minute, he stood motionless, gawking at the huge mass in front of him. Finally, he went into motion. He immediately began taking pictures from every possible angle, measured the length of the carcass, and took numerous hair and flesh samples.

"We have almost finished constructing a new lab at the university. We can actually use it now! All I have to do is make a few calls and the area will be secure within the hour! said Dr. Kluud.

"We'll have to fly this thing out. I think the National Guard can do it for us." said Gaines.

"Fly it to the northernmost wing of the campus. You'll see the helipad. The helipad will be out of sight of the students and the faculty. The new lab is right there, with a door that leads directly to the helipad. It is a secure place. My colleagues will be waiting, by the time you arrive." said Dr. Kluud.

Within an hour, a large National Guard helicopter hovered overhead. The creature was loaded into a shipping container and on its way to the university. Dr. Kluud, watched eagerly as the helicopter lifted off. This was a rare moment of his life, and he tried to savor it as much as he could. The U.S. Forest Service took every effort to keep radio transmissions discreet regarding Bernie's rescue incident and the creature that was being flown to the university. As far as the Service knew, the news media never intercepted their sparse radio communications regarding the dead creature.

The helicopter landed on the university's northern helipad, which was out of sight, just as the professor had said. U.S. Forest Service Rangers were already waiting to provide security. The professors of Zoology, Microbiology, Anthropology, and Veterinary Science were waiting to examine the creature. They were not informed as to why they were to secretly report to the northernmost wing.

"What was going on? The new lab was not even finished yet!" asked the professor of anthropology.

Although the professors were confused, they were anxious to see what was being brought to them. The staff watched eagerly as the helicopter lowered the worn out looking shipping container.

"What was inside of it? Why all the secrecy?" they wondered. The shipping container touched down on the snow-covered helipad. The professors quickly to ran the container. The door of the container was opened and the creature was quickly wheel out. The creature was hidden under several large white sheet. Within seconds, the sheet-covered carcass was inside the hall of the northern wing and being rushed down the short hall to the main examination room.

"I know you were given such short notice, but I think what you're about to see will make up for all the trouble! Secrecy is priority, does everyone understand?" asked Dr. Kluud.

Dr. Kluud slowly and carefully removed the white sheets from the creature. One of the professors of Zoology, Mrs. Brown, jumped backwards and gasped, knocking over a row of glass vials. The eyes of all of the other professors bulged out in stark surprise.

"Isn't it amazing?" laughed Dr. Kluud. None of the eight professors answered; instead, they just continued to stare at the creature lying before them.

The team went to work immediately to gather statistics on the new discover. The creature was placed in an examination room that was kept at thirty degrees. The dark room contained a mobile full-body CT scanner and numerous other laboratory machines. The dead creature lay on the examination table with three arrows still lodged in its body. The faculty members were required to sign a document of secrecy regarding the examination of the creature. Rangers Laski and Ranger Greer, were positioned in the hallway to restrict and monitor traffic. Ranger Rusty Gaines announced that no information was to be made public until he gave the permission to make the disclosure.

The first series of tests included samples of hair, skin, blood, and tissue samples for DNA analysis. As Dr. Kluud made a cursory examination of the creature, he spoke into his lapel microphone, which was attached to digital voice recorder in his laboratory coat.

"Sunday, December 20, . . . 5:05 PM. First audio recording. Upon a cursory observation of the specimen I notice that the black hair is extremely coarse, somewhat similar to that of a gorilla, but is much thicker and extremely long. At some parts of the body the hair is twenty-four inches long. The skin is dark grey and has several layers of fat. The muscle tissues are extremely dense, indicating that the creature has an immense amount of strength. Rigor mortis has not yet set in. The claws in the hands and feet black, hooked, nearly four inches long and nearly one inch in thickness at the base, and tapering to a sharp, curved, point. It is obviously a predator. Its face looks remotely similar to a gorilla, yet distinctively different. I have with me a fossilized lower jaw of the Gigantopithecus. By comparison, the jaw of today's specimen appears to be larger, wider, and has more teeth. Evidently, this specimen is not a Gigantopithecus, but something that hasn't been classified. There are canine teeth on both the upper and lower jaws, containing a total of thirty six teeth. The eyes are about four times as large as a human's eye. The pupils are round, like that of a man or of a primate. The irises are dark brown, almost black. The nostrils are remotely similar to that of gorilla, but longer and narrower. They are more of a virtual slit in comparison to a gorilla's nostrils. The ears are five inches long, pointed, indicating that it has great aural capacity. I did not witness its gate, but the citizen said that it walked towards him on two legs.

The creature is nine feet one inch in length and weighed in at 1109 pounds.

It appears to be a male. A complete analysis of the blood and tissue will be available in a couple of weeks.

Within a week, a folder containing nearly five hundred pages of medical statistics of the creature was compiled in a white folder labeled "Rocky Mountain Creature #1." It was designated as "#1" because it was black and a gray colored creature was supposedly still roaming the mountains. Dr. Kluud spent three sleepless days reading every page and adding his own notes regarding this unique discovery.

Chapter 6

The Lab Files

Within twenty-four hours after the dead creature was brought to the secret lab of the University of Colorado at Denver, nearly five hundred pages of medical statistics of the creature was compiled and placed in a white folder labeled "Rocky Mountain Creature #1. "It was designated as "#1" because the gray colored beast was still thought to be roaming the mountains. Professor Leo Kluud work meticulously as he compiled each page and made countless additions to his findings each hour.

Ricky was finally able to make his first visit to the see the dead specimen.

Ricky paused at the door before walking in see the specimen. An eerie, weird, and ghastly feeling overcame him as reaching for the doorknob. After nearly two nervous minutes, Ricky felt that he had enough composure to enter the room.

Ricky walked into the cold lab where the professor was sitting. He winced at the rank odor of the specimen lying on the examination table. It was not a smell of decay, but a smell of wildness. The smell was so foreign; he could not compare it to anything that he had known of. Ricky could only liken the smell of the creature to that of a dirty wet animal. It reminded him of his dog, but much worse.

"Oh the smell . . ." began Ricky.

"Dr. Kluud, how are things going?" asked Ricky.

"Smell?" giggled Dr. Kluud with obvious pleasure. "It is the smell of discovery! This is heaven for me! It's been years since I've been this excited!" said Leo.

"It's quite a discovery, isn't it!" said Ricky, trying to hide the nervousness that was starting to well up inside of him.

"You look nervous. Are you alright, Ricky?" asked Dr. Kluud. "Uh . . . yeah, of course . . ." Ricky stammered.

"You'll be okay! Just try to take it easy! I can assure you that it is truly dead. It's not going to hurt anyone!" smiled Dr. Kluud.

Ricky slowly walked over to get a better look at the massive black figure stretched out on the examination table. He felt a sudden fear and stopped walking as he got closer to the beast on the table. Suddenly Ricky felt waves of terror as he saw the beast lay motionlessly on the table.

Is this thing really dead? Ricky thought to himself. Ricky feared that the motionless creature would come to life, sit up, and reach out to grab him. After a few deep breaths, he felt his heartbeat return to normal, and he felt his composure return. The entire time, Leo watched Ricky, taking notice of the fear that Ricky was obviously feeling.

"Trust me. It is truly dead!" reassured Dr. Kluud.

What can tell me about this . . . thing?" asked Ricky.

"The creature is nine feet one inch tall, weighs 1109 pounds, and it appears to be a male." smiled Dr. Kluud.

Ricky slowly walked up to the table to look into the face of the bizarre beast. Ricky trembled as he looked at the creature's massive head. The facial features were like nothing that Ricky had ever encountered before. The face of the beast appear to so merciless, demonic, menacing, and completely inhuman. It was hard for Ricky to describe the face he was looking at. It looked somewhat like gorilla, but then again, it didn't.

"Is . . . this what a demon is supposed to look like?" asked Ricky.

"How should I know, Ricky?" smiled Dr. Kluud.

Ricky, turning his head from side to side, then said, "This can't be a primate."

"Maybe it can be. I would have to agree that it only faintly resembles a primate. I was hoping that what we have is a gigantopithecus, but its entire bone structure is completely different from the gigantopithecus fossils that was discovered a few years ago." said Leo.

Ricky noticed that the creature's enraged dark eyes were still wide open, as if it were determine to get its victim, or at least died trying to.

One thing that Ricky was sure about, though, is that the creature still looked furious, even though it was dead! The gaping jaws only magnified the eeriness of being so close to it. Its jaws were opened so wide that Ricky felt sure that his own head could fit into it, if it wasn't for the Bernie Lukey's arrow, which was still protruding from it. The creature had large three-inch-long canine teeth on both the top jaw and huge bottom jaw. Ricky could not see its cheeks since its entire face was covered in long, dark black hair that seemed to be radiating out from its small vertical nose slits.

"Just look at that huge, barrel chest! It's shaped like a football player, but with muscles, instead of plastic and foam pads!" Ricky remarked.

"Oh, I'd say that it is sturdily built!" laughed Leo.

The more you laugh, the more you resemble Santa Claus! Ricky thought within himself.

The creature's abdominal cavity was already opened and its internal organs were removed and being inspected. Ricky looked into the huge empty visceral cavity.

"I could easily fit inside his abdomen, don't you think?" asked Ricky.

"As big as that cavity is, I would think so!" smiled Dr. Kluud.

Ricky noticed that the skin at the edge of the incision was dark grey. He walked over to where the professor was sitting."What is this creature, Professor?" asked Ricky.

"You tell me, Ricky. Is it the same kind of creature that attacked you?" asked Leo.

"Yep . . . it's the same kind of creature, only this one is as black as the night!" replied Ricky.

"Professor, its cold in here!" said Ricky shivering.

"Its thirty degrees to be exact!" the professor responded, smiling. "We have to keep him fresh. We're going to deep freeze him in dry ice in a couple of days."

"Well Professor, what else can you tell me so far?"

"This is unlike anything that I have ever examined!" said Dr. Kluud with raised eyebrows. "For starters, an X-ray of the animal's head reveals that the cranium is nearly six inches thick in some areas and that its brain is remarkably small in relation to the size of its skull. The brain is only about the size of grapefruit."

"Yeah, I'd say that it's pretty small for a head this big!" remarked Ricky.

"The small size of the brain indicates to me the possibility that these creatures posses very little intelligence, like that of most animals. The X-ray images of the entire body proved to be quite a surprise! The creature walks upright like a human, but its skeleton is quite different. Its sternum is more than a foot wide and several inches thick. It completely covers and protects the heart." Leo added.

"So heart shots might not work." said Ricky.

"If you can break through that sternum, a heart shot should bring it down. The thick ribs extend lower than that of humans, and completely cover all of its vital organs. The scapulas are also several inches thick, are immensely broad, and completely cover the back of the lungs. You'll need a heavy hitting round to break through the sternum, ribs, or the scapulas." said Leo.

"Like a shotgun slug?" asked Ricky.

"I would think so." answered Leo.

In some areas of its body, the hairs are nearly thirty inches long. The muscles are unbelievably dense. There is a triple layer of fat under its skin.

"Do want to hear something very interesting?" asked Dr. Kluud.

"Sure!" replied Ricky.

"It has fingerprints." grinned Leo.

"What? Are you serious?" asked Ricky.

Ricky walked over to the massive, clawed hands of the creatures. The palms were down on the table. Ricky could only look at the top of the hands and the long black claws. "We found animal hair under its claws, possibly of that of a deer. It's probably more related to humans that to primates, because its bone structure is closer to that of a man than a primate. What is unusual is that it does not have both a radial and tibia, but one single bone connecting the elbow to the wrist. I found a deer's hoof and several pounds of deer flesh in its stomach. Its DNA is different from that of both man and primate. In my preliminary review of this creature's data, I really cannot establish its evolutionary connection between man and primate. It is a unique species altogether. If we could locate its den or see where it sleeps, our anthropologists would be able to provide more information about this beast." Professor, I came to take pictures of it. Would that be okay with you?"

"That would be fine, as long as you keep them confidential. We don't want to meet with the media just yet."

"I understand. Believe me; I don't want to deal with them either."

"Ricky, I really want to see if someone can bring in one of the creatures alive." The professor said bluntly.

Ricky looked at him for a brief moment then looked at the creature. After about a minute he cleared his throat. "Okay, we'll try.

"Leo, how many of these creatures do you think exists?"

"We may be down to one, now . . . the gray one that attacked you." replied the Dr. Kluud

Chapter 7

Lloyd

Under a full moon, the old green wagon slowly approached the old Green Leaf Bridge. As Lloyd drove along, he looked at his watch, 11:45 p.m. The old car began to sputter and shake. Suddenly the motor died and the car, coasted from twenty miles an hour to zero. Lloyd was able to pull the car off the road and onto a snowy shoulder before it came to a complete stop. The dashboard was still lit up. Lloyd looked at the instruments to see that the tank was half full, and the water temperature was normal.

"Oh Great! Absolutely great!" he shouted as he slammed from drive to park. It was the second time in two weeks that the car had died on him. Lloyd took out his cell phone, and became more irritated as he noticed that his battery was already dead. He looked around him for any sign of stores, gas stations, or anything at all. All he could see was the Green Leaf Bridge, brightly lit under the full moon. Over the bridge, perhaps five miles away, Lloyd could see the lights of Willow Township, a small community. He knew that it had a small motel, a few convenience stores, and even a bar, there. Behind him was nearly fifteen miles of the Rocky Mountain's forests, ridges, and valleys. He pulled his uncle's revolver out from under the driver's seat, placed it in his front pocket and stepped out of the car. Once he locked his car he began walking to the bridge. This was going to be a cold, five mile walk towards town. The full moon lit up the entire landscape with a blue light. He could literally see for miles around him. It was being to snow heavily and the wind began to blow moderately. He walked quickly to generate some heat. The fresh snow, nearly ankle deep, crunched under his feet with each step. The wooden bridge, nestle in a densely wooded area, was old, but well-maintained. The wide river beneath it had frozen over with ice thick enough that even a heavy man could walk across it. He was only about one minute away from the bridge when he had a haunting feeling that he was being. Perhaps it was wolves, or a bear, or some other kind of animal. Lloyd didn't know, but he had that gut feeling that something was wrong.

The creature stood high up on the ridge above him. It watched Lloyd step out of the old car. It decided that this would be an easy meal. Slowly it stalked its way down the ridge. Lloyd trudged twenty yards in the ankle deep snow towards the bridge. Lloyd suddenly noticed a strong smell that he was not familiar with. The strong odor was repulsive, like that of a wet, dirty dog. He looked around him and saw nothing but a falling snow, dense snow covered pine trees, and a blue winter landscape.

A minute later, as Lloyd stepped onto the old bridge, he heard the faint sound of the snapping of twigs on the ridge above him. Without stopping, he looked around him quickly, thinking that it may have been a deer. The continuing sound of breaking twigs became a little more audible with each second. Lloyd began to realize that the noise was getting louder and closer. *That doesn't sound right! Am I being followed?* he thought. Suddenly he realized that the sounds were constant and rhymic. The sounds were definitely footsteps on breaking twigs and leaves. Lloyd's anxiety quickly grew. He felt the hairs on his neck stand up as he realized the snapping of twigs was not moving away from him, but towards him from behind. He quickened his walk towards the bridge. He turned around repeatedly to see what was making the noise. The sound of the footprints breaking brush and twigs became deafening louder and much quicker. Whoever or whatever it was behind him was walking really fast, and getting really close. He placed his hand on his carried nickel plated revolver, which he had "borrowed" from his uncle. He turned to look behind him again.

"Who's there?" demanded Lloyd. There was no reply, but the continuing sound of quickly advancing footprints. Lloyd was certain that some kind of animal, probably black bear was stalking him. Looking over his shoulder as he walked, he drew out the revolver and held it as he made his way to the center of the old bridge.

"Come and get it!" he said, with arrogance, as he reached the bridge. There was no doubt about it, someone or something was obviously pursuing him. He was certain about it. The sounds of the breaking of brush became louder and determine. The sound of a large branches breaking was more than he could handle. Lloyd turned around, and pointed his revolver, in the direction of the noise.

"Oh my!" he said out loud as he saw the gray shaggy figure emerge from the dense cluster of snow-covered pine trees. The moon lit up the monster brightly. Lloyd could clearly see that it walked on two legs, well over eight feet tall, and perhaps four or five times broader than he was. Its shaggy gray coat blew in the wind. It had broad shoulders, thick arms, and huge belly. Lloyd could not make out its facial details. It was obviously not human. It was walking towards Lloyd at a fast pace. The creature stretched out its arms towards, let out a ear splitting roar, and reached out towards Lloyd with both arms, extending its clawed fingers. The sound of the angry roar was eerie and wild, unlike any cry of any animal he knew of. Lloyd, trembling, pointed the gun at the creature as he walked backwards across the bridge. The creature continued to walk swiftly towards Lloyd. Lloyd continued to walk backwards towards center of the bridge still pointing his gun at the creature. Lloyd's trembling hand finally squeeze the trigger. When the creature reached at the bridge, the first round flew from the gun. The round hit the deck a couple of feet in front of the creature. The second shot hit the handrail to the left of the creature. The third shot zipped passed the creature and hit somewhere in the trees. The fourth shot hit the deck in front the creature again. The fifth shot went past the creature. Finally the sixth shot hit somewhere on the creature's body. The creature flinched, let out a blood curdling howl, but continued to advance slowly towards Lloyd. The creature quickly regained a fast walking pace. Click! Click! Click! The revolver was empty! Lloyd quickly turned and ran as fast as he could. His hat flew off his head as he reached full speed. The creature also increased its gate and it began to run too. Within seconds, the creature's massive clawed feet stomped on the cap which fell from Lloyd's head. When Lloyd reached the opposite end of the bridge, he met a Ford Expedition coming towards. He ran to the passenger's side window and frantically knocked on the window. An old lady, who was driving, panicked at the sight of the pistol he had inadvertently pressed flat against her passenger window. She screamed in fear

"Lady help! Please let me in!" cried Lloyd.

The lady screamed again, still staring at the pistol he had in his hand. She slammed her foot on the gas pedal. The Expedition zoomed forward and raced down the bridge. The lady looked in hear mirror to see Lloyd just standing there looking at her. Suddenly as the old lady looked forward again, she saw a massive shaggy figure, illuminated by her headlights, standing in the middle of the both lanes. The creature roared and then lifted both arms towards the oncoming truck. The old lady screamed and then swerved to miss the creature. The Expedition broke through the wooden guard rail and plunged through the frozen river beneath. The old lady screamed in panic as the felt the truck turn over and sinks under the ice.

Within seconds, the truck was completely submerged under the sheets of ice.

Lloyd stood in terror as he saw the massive grey shaggy creature walking quickly towards him. He dropped his revolver in the snow and ran down the road. After a mile, he began to slow to an exhausted trot, continually, looking over his shoulder for the beast. Lloyd stopped and stood, bowed over due to exhaustion. He tried to listen intently through the sound of his gasping for air, for any sounds of the creature. He could hear the creature's roar. He trembled with fear, when he realized that the roar wasn't far behind him. The creature gave out a medium pitched thunderous wail, unlike anything that could come out of the throat of any human. Suddenly in the distance, he could see the huge gray figure trotting towards him. Lloyd turned and began another sprint. This time, he could only sprint about 300 yards before he came stumbling to ground on the side of the road. He quickly got up to look behind him. The silhouette was still following him closely behind him. He knew he had to keep moving! He continued to run another 200 yards. His heart was pounding, his lung burned, he was fighting for air. His legs were becoming tight and heavy. He was drenched with sweat. The creature continued on its course. Lloyd knew that to stay was to die. He started a new sprint for another 200 yards in the darkness. As he ran he saw drainage tube that came out under the road. He headed for it. Lloyd's heart nearly burst out of his chest as he ran for his life. He left the road, climbed down the embankment and headed for the drainage hole. He dove in, practically headfirst, and scrambled in as fast as hand, knees, and feet could move him. He was able to squeeze himself around to look at the opening to see the creature reaching its massive arm inside, frantically trying to grab whatever part of Lloyd that it could. It reached in vain; Lloyd was only two yards beyond its reach, and the creature was too big to enter! Although Lloyd was safe, he was still filled with terror, as the beast continued to roar and wail at him.

What kind of beast was it? Worst of all, it was out to get him! The creature continued to grope and grab for fifteen long minutes. Finally it stuck its shaggy head in to look at Lloyd. Due to the darkness, Lloyd could not see the face, but only the silhouette of its massive shaggy head. It's deafening, indescribably roar, somewhat like that of a tiger, thundered in the tight space of the tube. Finally, after what seemed an eternity, the creature slowly backed its head out. It turned away from the drainage tube walked away into the moonlight night. Lloyd looked at his immensely wide shoulders and thick shaggy back. Floyd watched it as it walked away. It was big, really big, and obviously too big to be human. Within a minute, it disappeared behind the snow covered trees, in front of the tube. Floyd was finally able to breathe a sigh of relief. He felt that the best thing to do was to wait for sunrise. Before he knew it, it was already 7am in the morning. Lloyd laughed within himself. He never knew that the day would come when he would have to run for his life from a wild animal or whatever that thing was. He never knew that he would wake up in the refuge of drainage tube under a road. He sat up within the drainage tube. He thought to himself; *How he was going to explain to his boss the reason why he was late for work?* Would his boss believe him? *Of course not! I probably won't make it to work until lunchtime.* He shook his head in disbelief and hopelessness. He looked at the opening of the drainage tube. An uneasy feeling entered his gut as he stared at the opening of the tube. *Is safe for me to go out?* He though. He stared intently into the distance for any signs of movement. All he could see was a light steady snowfall. An hour had passed.

I can't stay in here forever! He thought. He developed a plan. He decided to quietly creep to the opening of the drainage tube to get a wider view of the area. He would just go far enough to look out, but not too far, in case he needed to quickly back up into the tube. If there was no sign of the creature, he would dash up the road, and sprint into Willow Township. As quietly as he could, he crawled to the opening of the tube.

Lloyd looked around. Snow, rocks, trees, snowfall . . . . no creature!

Good! He thought. Slowly he crawled completed out of the drainage tube. Unbeknownst to him, the creature was standing directly above the drainage tube! Without a sound, it reached down and grabbed him by the back of his neck and lifted him straight up into the air. In horror Lloyd tried to scream but couldn't since the creatures hand had squeezed so tightly around his neck. Lloyd felt the massive black claws sink deep within his throat. Lloyd felt the claws of the other hand drive deep into the side and his abdomen. Within minutes, the creature had eviscerated and devoured him, leaving his bloody remains in the middle of the road.

Chapter 8

Deputy Mills

At the close of some news regarding a union strike, the news caster announced,

"Breaking News, the remains of a man was discovered by motorist this morning, on Sampson River Road near the Green Leaf Bridge. Our field reporters are on scene with an update.

"Thank you Clay! This is Franklin Aberst reporting live from the Sampson River Road, near the Green Leaf Bridge. This morning the Sheriff's department arrived to this location behind me, because they were notified of a grisly discovery. Apparently the remains of a man were found in the middle of the narrow two lane highway about half an hour ago. It is suspected that a bear is responsible for the attack. As you can see, deputies and investigators are on scene behind me. The deputies say that have discovered large footprints, possibly a bear, leading up and even away from the remains. Sheriff Deputies using canines are currently following the footprints. The Sampson River Road leading from Willow Township is closed until further notice. Drivers are advised to us Farrow Road which parallels Sampson River Road. "Deputy, can you tell us more about the incident?" asked the reporter.

"At this time we have few details to offer you other than that a body was discovered in the road. We were able to confirm the identity of the victim but his name will not be disclosed until we first contact his immediate family. We'll provide a statement at a later time." he replied and abruptly walked away.

"We'll keep you updated as new details are provided by the Sheriff's Department. For Channel Seven news, this is Franklin Aberst. Goodbye." said the reporter.

Nearby, some of the customers at Claude's Diner, who were watching the wall mounted television, looked at each other in disbelief.

"What?" asked an old truck driver, as he looked across the table to his partner.

"A bear attack, huh? I think we better take a different highway outa' this place!" replied the partner.

Ricky Toomis was sitting at his table eating breakfast while watching the breaking news.

Oh no! Now it's going after humans! thought Ricky, as he dropped his fork onto the plate. Waves of terror raced through him as he watched the news broadcast. He sat for a few minutes as he mind went back to his own encounter with the gray beast. He remembered how that the first thing he set his eyes on was the cavernous mouth, dark eyes, and the deafening ear piercing roar of the monster. He began to tremble in his chair.

A few minutes later, his cell phone rang.

"Hello?" answered Ricky.

"Officer Toomis? Sir, this is Deputy Midge Mills of the Lassiter County Sheriff's Department. How are you this morning?" asked Mills.

"Oh . . . I've seen better days, Deputy Mills. How can I help you?" replied Ricky.

"Sir, like everyone else, our department was notified that you were assault and I just wanted to get a couple of small details to give us a better idea of what we are dealing with. Do you have few a minutes to speak with me?"

"Absolutely, go ahead Sir!" replied Ricky.

"Our CSI team photographed the footprints leading up to and even leaving the incident scene. The Sheriff's department received a forwarded email of the photographs of the footprints of your attacker. The pictures of the footprints that we took and the ones sent from the U. S. Forest Service us are similar. Officer Toomis, was it a brown bear or black bear?

"Bear? Ummm . . . it wasn't a bear. It was some kind of a creature." replied Ricky.

What's this guy saying? Okay . . . this guy is on hospital painkillers! thought Mills.

"Can you please describe to me what you saw?" asked Mills

"Well, it was big. I am guessing may eight to nine feet tall. It was wide, maybe five to six feet across. It had a big barrel chest and it looked really heavy. Mean or angry-looking face."

Deputy Mills frowned and looked across the ceiling as he listened intently to the phone. *"Yeah . . . whatever!"* Mills thought, shaking his heading in disbelief.

"Like a man or gorilla?" Mills ventured.

"Yes . . . well, no. It vaguely looked like a man or gorilla, but it looked different. It's hard to describe. All I can say is that it had big fangs on the top and bottom. It roared or wailed at me, really loudly, like I had really ticked it off!"

"Really? And what did that sound like?" said Mills.

"Like a lion, well . . . sort of . . . it's hard to explain." replied Ricky. *Yeah, I'll bet it's hard to explain! Your story getting worse by the minute!* thought Mills. "It was hairy, or shaggy, dirty looking. It stank so badly!"

"It stank?" asked Mills.

"Smelled like some dirty dog, but ten times worse." said Ricky. "What color jacket was this . . . thing? Light gray, medium gray, dark gray, or what?" asked Mills.

"Gray, like ash." replied Ricky.

"Ash gray?" asked Mills.

"Yes, ash gray." replied Ricky.

"Could it have been a man in a monkey suit?" asked Mills.

Ricky thought for a minute, not knowing how to answer the question.

What a jerk! thought Ricky.

"Mr. Toomis, are you there?" asked Mills

"Yes, I'm here. Sir, I don't think it was a guy wearing a suit." replied Ricky.

"Officer Toomis, I understand this thing grabbed you?" asked Mills.

75

"It either tried to grab me or took a swing at me. I'm not sure. The next thing I knew, I was lying in this hospital bed." said Ricky.

"From the report we got, it sounds like he . . . or it was out to steal your horse!" said Mills.

"Maybe so." replied Ricky.

Wait a minute, this cop still thinks I was assaulted by a man! thought Ricky.

"Do you have an official report you can fax to me?" asked Mills.

"Yes, I'll call the office and have the records technician fax it you. Is it the same fax number, as it was before?"

"Yes, it is still the same." replied Mills.

"You'll have it within the hour." said Ricky.

"Perfect! Hey listen, I really appreciate your help in this matter!" said Mills.

"Hey, no problem. Please do me a favor. Please fax me what you have, on your investigation of that body that was discovered, since we may be dealing with same creature. Can you do that?" asked Ricky.

Creature? thought Mills.

"Our course! I may be calling you again soon, or meeting with you within a couple of days." said Mills.

"That will be fine!" said Ricky.

"Hey, take it easy, I know you'll still recovering. We'll work together, and he'll have your man as soon as possible." said Mills.

My man? thought Ricky.

"I hope so. Take care. Goodbye!" said Mills trying his best to be agreeable.

"Bye!" replied Ricky.

Crazy ranger! Where do they get these guys from? thought Mills.

Ricky sat for a minute, staring out the window. *Great, I got a cop who thinks it's a man that attacked me!* thought Ricky. He stared off into the distant snow-covered mountains. He reached for his cellular phone.

"Leo, it's me Ricky!" said Ricky.

"Good morning Ricky!" replied Leo, cheerfully as usual.

"Have you seen the news, yet? Our little secret is no longer a secret." Ricky said gravely.

"I've seen the news! I know it. We need to capture it quick, before it takes another victim." said Leo.

"Capture it? No . . . I think we'll have to kill it!" said Ricky.

"No Ricky, please! We must take it alive! I have a plan!" pleaded Leo.

"A plan? What is your plan?" asked Ricky.

"There is someone I want you to meet." replied Leo.

Chapter 9

Broken Glass

Julie Blackhawk was a pretty twenty-year-old, Native American young woman. She was of the Yemanache tribe that lived along the western Canadian shoreline. Working at the Big Flower Convenience store part-time, allowed her to a little bit of extra spending change to enjoy while being a student. Her work shift began at 11:00 P.M. and ended 7:00AM, on Mondays, Wednesdays, and Fridays. She was busy, stocking the coolers with milk, sodas, sports drinks, and, cold coffees. Usually she would have the shelves and the cooler stocked and filled by 2:00 A.M. What she enjoyed most about working at Big Flower Convenience Store was that she could get her school work done during the midnight shift. She would then set up her laptop, open her Biology book and Medical Terminology book, and study until 5:00 A.M., with only a few interruptions from customers. Big Flower Convenience Store sat about 1 mile outside of the City of Lassiter, Colorado. The Rocky Mountains were only a few hundred yards to the west of the back of the store. On a couple of occasions she saw a mountain lion and even a black bear. What she was going to see this evening was going to total change her world. Julie really enjoyed working at this convenience store. Her goal was to someday be a nurse. At 2:15 A.M., an older man, perhaps fifty years old, walked in. He wore an old black baseball cap, old brown snow jacket, blue jeans, and snow boots. "Pack of Marlboro, please!" he kindly asked. After paying for the cigarettes he said, "I think I might need something else." The man walked over to clothing rack, near the cash register and began examining the different snow gloves and colorful winter stocking caps hanging there. "I need something better than this old cap of mine!" he said amiably.

Julie looked up occasionally from her textbook to see the man trying on different hats and gloves. Suddenly and without warning, the window where he was standing imploded, sending broken glass flying across the floor and near the cash register. The violence and the loud sound of the breaking glass started Julie, causing her to scream and fall backwards against the wall behind her. She instinctive placed her hands in front of her eyes to shield them from the flying glass. When she brought her hands down, she saw the abnormally large, shaggy arms reaching for customer. The massive arms grabbed the man by the neck, and lifted him off of the floor. Julie let out bone shaking scream as she watched the man eyes bulge wide open. The horrified man, gagged and tried to scream, but there was too much pressure around his throat to allow any air to come out of his mouth. The shaggy arms then quickly jerked the man through the window, breaking more glass as the man's body was pulled through it. The man's body instantly vanished into the blackness of night. Julie let out another chilling scream as she stared at the shattered window.

After what may have been several minutes, her trembling hand hit the red emergency alarm, under the cash register. She stayed in the corner, near the register, trembling, wondering if the unknown creature would return for her next. She couldn't go outside, since she was one mile from the city. It was too dark, too snowy, and that thing was probably nearby! She could only wait in the corner and stare at the broken window. An eternally long ten minutes passed. She felt some comfort as she saw the flashing red and blue lights of the sheriff's cars coming down the snowy highway. The deputies ran in.

"What happened, ma'am?" asked Deputy Midge Mills. He stood nearly six feet tall, brown eyes, and a dark mustache.

Deputy Mills was a former Army Military Police Officer. He joined the Sheriff's department at the end of his Army stint, when he was twenty-three-years old. Now at twenty-seven years old, he had the confidence, or arrogance, that he could take on the world. He was single, determined, confident, aggressive, arrogant, often, downright rude.

Deputy Mills quickly scanned Julie, from head to toe, looking for any obvious signs of injury. Not seeing any injuries, he began a quick investigation.

"How was the window broken?" he asked

"It..it reached it arm in through the glass and took a customer away! I..I don't know what it was!" stammered Julie.

"What reached in? A man, a bear, or what?" asked Mills.

"No, it..it was big . . . a big hairy arm . . . with fingers!" she continued.

Miles, obviously puzzled, looked at her his partner and then looked at Julie.

"Deputy, do think . . . ." Mills began to speak, but paused in mid sentence. Deputy Mills looked at the broken window, glass covered floor, blood, and then quickly scanned the room.

"Are you saying a person was abducted?" he asked.

"Yes, it took a customer!" Julie sobbed.

Mills ran outside of the convenience store to examine the broken window. Shining his flashlight down, he saw drops of blood, and even more interestingly, abnormally huge footprints!

"Oh, my! Same big footprints!" Mills said to himself.

Mills walked back inside the store.

"Ma'am, if you would, play the video for us to see!" said Mills.

Julie reached her trembling hand under the register, and worked the controls on the video recorder.

"Deputy Feltzer, watch the tape! I've got to get onto those footprints!" said Mills. Within minutes two more deputy patrol cars arrived, along with the paramedics. The crime scene tape was stretched out. Other deputies began a more detailed interview with Julie. Deputy Mills looked around to see who was available to give him assistance.

"You four, go with me!" ordered Mills. Four deputies, including Mills, turned on their flashlights and began the arduous trek up the ridge, following the massive footprints. The hike proved difficult from the very start. It was a steep upward angle, without any worn path to follow, through ankle deep, sometimes knee deep snow. It was a dark moonless night. The only light they had was their flashlights. The wind blew extremely hard, and the snowfall quickly increased. The deputies found themselves going uphill over unseen rocks and tree roots. Progress was slow and tiring. This quickly proved to be difficult work out.

"Sky One . . . Delta 19" radioed one of the Mills.

"Go for Sky One." came the reply.

"Can you meet us at Lantern Mountain Peak?" asked Mills. "10-4 . . . ETA fifteen minutes." came the reply. This offered some hope for the men. Hopefully the incoming Sheriff's helicopter could provide assistance in spotting the alleged attacker. The men were about ten minutes into the hike, and they were already gasping for breath.

"Whoever or whatever it was, had at least thirty minutes of lead time on us. Hopefully we'll be able to run him down. I hope you boys are in shape for this!" said Mills.

"Mills, I'll bet you money, that I'm in better shape than you!" remarked another deputy.

"Hah! We'll see about that!" scoffed Mills. After nearly twenty minutes of grueling upward hiking through the windy, snowy, rocky ridges, the men paused for a two minute break.

"Delta 19, this is Sky One, could you shine your lights at me for a reference?" asked the pilot. Immediately, all the deputies shined their lights at the approaching helicopter.

"Got it! Thanks!" came the reply over the radio. From the air, the pilot could see a string of five lights against the dark, dimly lit snowy mountain side. Within a minute, the helicopter arrived, the pilot turned on his spot light and scanned the area around and ahead of the team of deputies. The powerful spotlight from the helicopter lift up a circular area, nearly ten meters in diameter, wherever it shined.

"Sky One, we got the footprints, right here, just keep going north, up the ridge. That's the direction the tracks are heading, directly north!" said Mills.

"Good copy, Delta 19" replied the pilot. The pilot hovered about one forty meters above the ground and slightly ahead of the deputies, scanning ahead and around the deputies for anything that moved.

"Sky One, do you have anything on infra red?" asked Mills."Standby!" replied the pilot. After about ten minutes, the pilot finally replied.

"Delta 19, be advised, I scanned ahead and around you and I've got nothing!"

"Good copy. We still have the tracks going straight north, up the ridge!" said Mills. After nearly another thirty minutes of fruitless pursuit and search, the pilot decided it was time to bring his vehicle home. He was unable to spot any movement around the men, or anywhere in the snow covered rocks and trees on the mountain.

"Delta 19 be advised . . . I am low on fuel and returning to base." said the pilot.

Oh no! thought Mills. The other deputies shared the same dismay. Helicopter assistance was a great help in this blizzard. They were sad to see it go.

"10-4 . . . Thanks for the assistance!" replied the deputy. The men sadly watched as the helicopter fly off into the distance. The men stopped the upward ascent and sat in a tight circle on a flat rock shelf. The men were gasping for air and were drenched with sweat. The snow continually to fall heavily and the wind increased dramatically. After about two minutes, the deputies sat shivering as their body temperature began to come down.

"Man, I think I'm gonna' frostbite in my fingers and toes!" complained Mills, as he tapped his boots together, trying to knock the snow and ice off of them. They rested for minute and then continued their upward trek.

"Guys, we've got to keep going, we're almost at the top!" encouraged Mills. This was not encouraging for the deputies. They were getting concerned for their own safety. The temperature had dropped into the twenties, they were drenched with sweat, the wind was blowing unmercifully, and the wind and snow was making visibility difficult.

"We'll freeze up here! We're soaking wet!" yelled a deputy. "Shut up! We're almost at the top! It's time to move!" barked Mills. The men unwilling got up and obeyed the order. They began the trek up the steep slope, following the footprints, which were starting to get filled in with fresh snow.

"Well, we'd better find that guy quick, before the fresh snow fills in these footprints!" argued the deputy again. Mills became extremely irritated at the deputy's complaining and decided it might be best to ignore him. The men were within about half an hour of reaching the peak. Although they could still see the footprints, the snow was quickly filling them in. All the while, the wind blew mercilessly, and the heavy snowfall worsened. Just before reaching the top of the ridge, due to the heavy snowfall, the footprints became very had to see. The men finally reached the rocky summit of Lantern Mountain, gasping desperately as they topped out onto its peak. There, to their confusion and dismay, the footprints disappeared! The deputy was right. The snow heavy snowfall had filled in the footprints. The were now at the top of Lantern Mountain, and the suspect was probably very close by. At the center of the mountain peak was a dense cluster of tall, snow covered pines. Looking around the pines were small trees and rocks, not tall enough to hide a man.

"He's in there!" said Mills, pointed his flashlight into the circular cluster of trees, about the size of a small parking lot. Mills drew out his pistol. The other deputies also drew out theirs. "Take cover!" ordered Mills. As best as the deputies could, the men got behind any rock or tree trunk that could provide cover.

Police! Come out with your hands up!" yelled Mills. Mills and the team waited for nearly three minutes. There was no response.

"Police! Come out with your hands up!" repeated Mills. They waited another three minutes.

"Forward, side by side, six feet between each man!" whispered Mills into his radio. The team of deputies obeyed and they slowly advanced, crouching low. Within seconds they reached the cluster of pine trees. Although no one admitted it, each deputy was filled with apprehension. They knew they were within feet of a killer and the situation was getting tense. Mills carefully pushed his way through snow covered branches, expecting to be struck with an object or shot by the suspect. His breath quickened and his heart raced. Mills, like each of the other four deputies, had an uneasy feeling that something really bad was about to happen. Things could go really wrong, really quick! The deputies slowly and carefully began to look behind every tree and rock that was large enough to hide a man.

The sky was moonless, they had no light other than their flashlights, they were pushing their way through thick branches, and visibility was limited. Fifteen minutes later, the deputies were sure that they had searched behind every tree that could possibly hide a man. No one was found. The deputies carefully searched the snow for tracks around the circular cluster of trees. No footprints could be seen. The men then searched every area where the suspect could have come down from the peak. They found no footprints, no broken tree limbs, no snapped twigs, no evidence of any disturbance of the snow or the brush. Nothing. After nearly an hour, they decided it was time to quit. One of the deputies, feeling dehydrated grabbed handfuls of snow and began to eat it. The other deputies soon followed. Mills looked around and shook his head. "He's not in this patch of trees. He must have gone back down. But which way?" asked Mills.

The other deputy simply shook his head side-to-side, indicating that they didn't know.

"No way! Where could he have gone down?" asked Mills.

"I knew it! I knew it! The snow would fill in all the tracks!" sighed the deputy.

"Yeah . . . yeah, I guess you were right." said Mills.

The men looked around at the moonless, dark, snowy, mountainous expanse. It would be a long forty-five minute hike down.

Chapter 10

The Video Recording

At the Sheriff's substation, Deputy Feltzer inserted the tape into the VHS player as Deputy Mills and Deputy Clay sat down in the chairs in front of the television screen.

"Okay, hopefully the picture quality will be good enough, this time, where we can get a good look at this guy." stated Deputy Clay.

"Yep!" agreed Deputy Mills. To their displeasure, the quality of the tape was less than desirable.

"Do all convenience stores have to have lousy security videos like this?" asked Feltzer, shaking his head. The camera angle and lighting was perfect. The entire store, as well as the area outside of the window that was broken was very brightly lit. The camera was aimed at the cash register and at the window that was broken.

"Good area coverage, but the video isn't focused and is too grainy." remarked Clay. The men didn't have to wait long to see what had happened. What they discovered on the tape was rather alarming although hard to make out. Within thirty seconds of playing the video, the video footage showed the fuzzy frontal image of the extremely tall, broad, gray, body walk up the large window. The deputies were barely able to see the long gray shaggy hair get whipped around by the wind. The deputies could clearly see the customer look up from the merchandise he was holding to look out at the gray figure on the other side of the window. Suddenly a thick shaggy, gray arm burst through the window, sending a burst of glass into the store.

"Stop the video!" said Mills.

Feltzer quickly hit the pause button.

"Did that guy just break that window with his fist?" asked Clay. "It looks like it. It looks like he just punched through it. The picture is so out of focus, I can't make out what he had in his and. He's got no tool or anything in his hand! It could be that he was high on drugs." replied Feltzer.

"Hit play!" order Mills. The deputies watched in surprise as the hand latched onto the man's throat and lifted him straight up from the floor.

"He's got to be at least six feet four." said Clay. The arm held him there for about two seconds, and then, quickly yanked him through the huge open circle of broken glass. Deputy Clay rewound the video several times for both of them to view. The deputies stared intently at the out of focus, grainy video.

"He was weary some shaggy gray coat, or a coat that was all beat to shreds." said Feltzer, as he was rubbing his chin.

"It almost looks like he's wearing a football uniform. Look how wide his shoulders are!" said Clay.

"He's got a wide build on him . . . a big weight-lifting dude." said Feltzer. The massive gray figure disappeared from the camera view and into the black snowy night. They watched the video over and over again trying to catch every possible detail of the crime. What bothered Deputy Clay the most the horrendous quality of the recording.

"I sure wish these convenience stores would stop using the same cheap video systems!" complained Feltzer.

"Well, let's look at the tape of the outside of the store." said Feltzer. To their dismay, the video of the outside of the store was even worse. The second showed the area in front of the window. Suddenly, the video displayed the entire front view of the suspect as it walked up to the window. It was amazing huge, broad and shaggy.

"Look how big that guy is!" remarked Feltzer.

"He looks shaggy!" asked Clay.

"Now that is a weird style of jacket. It's a parka." said Mills. "Did you see that, the dude grabbed him by the neck and just picked him off the ground!"

"Well, so much for the videos! We couldn't get a look at his face. We can't determine his ethnicity. All we know is that he is at least 6 feet four and he has a large build." said Clay as he walked out.

Chapter 11

Herbert Lear

Herbert Lear was an unmarried and well-respected Border Patrol Agent in El Paso Texas for ten years. He wasn't very tall, standing only about five feet five, but he had a big reputation. He had undisputedly the highest numbers of apprehensions than any other agent at his station. He was forced to medically retire due to vehicle accident which nearly claimed his life. During a high speed pursuit of a suspected drug vehicle, he had lost control of his pursuit sedan around a curve, broke through the barrier, and tumbled his vehicle down a ravine. The seat belt kept him alive, but he still suffered multiple injuries including partial loss of the use of his left arm. He still regularly visited a local indoor firing range to maintain his shooting skills with his right hand, which were still quite good. He could no longer work as a field agent but was permitted to work in the Intelligence Agent at the station. His new assignment paid the bills and offered him a secure retirement, but it lacked the excitement he once loved, out in the field. He could no longer participate in long foot chases through the mountains, vehicle stops, fist fights, apprehensions, drug busts, and other pleasantries of Border Patrol field work.

After becoming the Intelligence Agent, Herbert spent day after day, week after week, month after month, providing analysis information, writing correspondences, and providing other logistical support. Life had lost its luster and had become mundane. He longed for the days that he was out in the field, playing cat and mouse with illegal aliens. He longed the chase, the capture, the name of being the best at his station. Now, he could only hear about the "war stories" the other Border Patrol Agents had offer, and the end of their shift. He was sad, because those war stories used to be his own.

Now he had no more to share. Each time new Border Patrol trainees arrived at the station, he felt a person sense of loss. He loved seeing their enthusiasm, but he could no longer be part of the action. He often felt sad, but hid it well under his smile. He was getting restless. He had too much energy to be stuck in an office for the next twenty years of his life. Herbert Lear was intrigued upon seeing the news article regarding the alleged monster attack of Lassiter Colorado. As a teenager, he was fascinated about reports of supposed mysterious animals. He even wrote a report for his high school English teacher on the subject of crypto zoology. Because the alleged attack involved the disappearance and possible death of a person, he felt that this was an opportunity he could not pass up. He had an idea. He decided to take a "vacation." He didn't tell anyone what his real intentions were. People don't normal take a vacation to kill a legend. He couldn't because he didn't want to be the joke of his workplace. As far as his coworkers knew, Hebert was just going to take a couple of weeks of annual leave to relax. But his actual plans were big and possibly dangerous. He decided that it would be better that he kept his plans secret, and then come home with a huge trophy. With his skills he had honed in tracking illegal aliens, he felt confident that he could track down this supposed monster, find it, and bring it, dead or alive. He had the tracking skills, the cunning, and the nerve to try this stunt. This would surely bring break the mundane routine for him. It may even bring some fame and of course, some fortune with it! He had to be the one to bring it in to bring it in, first. He immediately put in for a "vacation" and jumped on the next flight to Denver.

His equipment consisted of a handheld Infra-Red telescope, which he had bought on the internet, a 30-06 caliber rifle, and a .50 caliber Desert Eagle, and a police knife. In his backpack he carried water, DVD video recorder, some flares, two LED flashlights, energy bars, binoculars, and toilet paper. *This should be enough!* He figured.

For three days Herbert scoured the snow-covered ridges within ten miles of the Big Flower Convenience Store looking for footprints and or any sign of the alleged creatures. Finally one the fourth day he struck gold! It hardly snowed at all that day. The sky was blue all day. It was a winter paradise. At six o'clock in the evening, while walking up a ridge, two miles west of the Big Flower Convenience Store he discovered the tracks. His jaw dropped and his eyes bulged at the sight of his discovery. A torrent of excitement filled his entire being. "Oh-ho-ho!" he laughed. The tracks were fresh! He pulled out tape measure and discovered the footprint to be twenty inches long. Herbert had to take two strides to equal one of the strides of whatever left these tracks. The imprint of clawed toes was clearly visible in the shallow snow. He judged that tracks to be less than hour old. He knew that if he ran, he would be able to catch up with the creature. His rifle was on "hot standby" so he chambered a round. His pistol, however, was ready to fire. He swallowed a few huge gulps of water, and began the chase northward. Within thirty minutes, the sun was down and there was a half moon. He pulled out his Infra-Red telescope for a quick survey of the area. Nothing. He continued to follow the tracks along the northward heading ridge. Fifteen minutes later the tracks led to a rock waterfall. The tracks ended where the rocks began. The creature had walked or leaped from rock to rock. As any Border Patrol Agent knew, trying to identify footprints on a rocky area was going to be tricky. After five minutes, he lost the tracks. He couldn't figure out if the creature had continued in a straight northerly direction, or had veered west or east. He stopped, pulled out in Infra-Red and scanned the area.

The hot spot was approximately 100 yards ahead of him. He ran towards it, dodging branches and jumping over rocks as he went. As Herbert Lear leaped over a rock, his arm hit a branch which knocked the Infra-Red device out of his hand. The IR slammed against a large rock, which shattered the lens. A wave of panic flooded his entire being as he saw the huge hole where the lens used to be. Now, the only thing that he could rely on to see what was around him was the moonlight! He could hear the breaking of branches on both his left side and right side. A new wave of fear flooded his body as he realized that there wasn't just one creature, but two. *Didn't I just see one hot spot!?* He could see fairly well under the half-moon, but he couldn't see that fact that both creatures were actually stalking the same prey, namely him! The creature on his left side let out deafening roar. Herbert quickly pointed his rifle toward it, but could not get a visual on any shape or form amongst the trees. The creature on the opposite side let out a throaty howl as if responding to the first. Herbert quickly spun around and pointed his rifle at the second noise but could see anything except snow-covered trees. The moonlight night gave Herbert good visibility, but he really had a greater advantage with his Infar-Red device. *"If I only had that IR!"* he thought. He heard the sound of branches breaking behind so he quickly spun around and pointed his rifle at it. This time could faintly see some kind of movement. He placed his front sight on it and fired. He waited. Ten seconds passed. He saw nothing. Suddenly from his left flank he could hear more branches breaking. He turned, pointed his front sight on it, and fired. He waited. Silence. He walked in the direction of his second shot. Suddenly from in front of him and behind him he could hear the sound of breaking branches and footsteps crunching in the snow. Herbert panicked realizing that two beasts were coming at him from opposite sides. Herbert raised his pistol and fired a double tap into the blackness in front of him. Both creatures reached him at about the same time. Herbert felt the long black nails of four hands as they lifted him off of the ground. Both creatures began pulling violently on him. Hebert felt a sharp pain as left arm was avulsed. Somehow he was still able to fire off more rounds. He wildly fired eight rounds into the shaggy mass in front of him. One round went through the middle of the creature's neck.

The creature behind Herbert then began to violently shake Hebert's body left and right. The force of the violent shaking sent his pistol flying off and landing into the snow. Herbert was hopelessly caught in the creature's firm grasp. He quickly lost consciousness due to blood loss. Within seconds there were two dead bodies on that snowy mountain, Herbert's, and one of the creatures.

Chapter 12

At a Coffee Shop with Leo

Dr. Leo Kluud and Troy Bellingmay sat cozily near the window in a local coffee shop at a shopping mall. Leo, as always, was dressed in the same attire that he taught his lectures in, dress slacks, shirt and tie, and old sport coat. Troy, as usual, wearing blue jeans, tan work boots, and long sleeve plaid shirt. Leo looked out the window to see the full moon and a busy sidewalk of Christmas shoppers. The coffee shop was packed full, the lights were low, and there were no more available tables. Leo felt that amidst the music and conversations, nobody would really take notice of what he and Troy were discussing.

"It's the Christmas season!" announced Leo.

"The hairy monster is waiting for the reindeer to arrive!" joked Troy.

"You think so?" laughed Leo.

"He'll get a sleeping dart for a Christmas gift!" boasted Troy.

"My, my, what a confident little boy we have here!" smiled Leo.

"Uncle Leo, if we can capture this animal, can you imagine what kind of shake up it will cause for the world?" asked Troy.

Leo sipped his mug of coffee and then gingerly set it down onto the wooden table.

"In regards to the studies of paleontology, anthropology, zoology, and every other 'ology', I agree that it'll be quite a shake up!" laughed Leo.

"Troy, can you see the significance of what we have here? Can you imagine what the world will say? You'll be the one credited for tranquilizing it, and I'll have first priority on the care of it and study of it! It's not fame or fortune that I am looking for, but it is the opportunity to study the greatest discovery of the century and contribute my findings to the annals of science! If we capture this creature, I'll be able to give the greatest work I have ever given to the scientific community! It would crown my final years as a paleontologist! This is a monumental opportunity the both of us!" he exclaimed enthusiastically.

"Yeah . . . yeah." replied Troy, as he stirred his own coffee. Actually, Troy was temporarily lost in thought, and hardly paying attention to what his uncle was saying. Troy was thinking about how he would look on the front cover of magazines.

"If we can get this beast, we'll be on front cover of 'Hunting Magazine' and other magazines!" said Troy.

"Perhaps, Troy! Are you ready for that kind of publicity?" laughed the professor.

"Oh yeah!" laughed Troy.

"What amount of the tranquilizer will you use?" asked the professor.

"I measured the dosage for approximately 1100 pounds of body weight, equal to the weight of the specimen you have in your lab. I think that dosage should bring it down without killing it." replied Troy.

"I sincerely hope you're right, kiddo!" laughted Leo. Leo sipped from his coffee mug thoughtfully for a few minutes. "Troy, I've been thinking about something." said Leo, breaking the silence.

"What is it?" asked Troy.

"What if the gray creature that attacked the ranger and the dead one at university's lab are the last of their kind? asked Leo.

"Uncle Leo, I hope that they aren't the last of their kind. We don't have a guarantee of it. It would be tragedy if we were the cause of their extinction." said Troy.

"That would be both an embarrassment and a tragedy for me, personally." replied the Leo.

"One thing that greatly concerns me is what the ranger or the deputy may do it. I'm sure they won't hesitate to kill the creature if it spooks them. I am very concerned about that." said Leo.

"Well you know cops. They're just itching to shoot someone or something." said Troy cynically.

"Now, now, I wouldn't go that far!" laughed the professor.

"How do you plan on shooting the creature, yourself?" asked Leo.

"I don't know yet. I'm still working out the plans for that. All I can say at this point is that I just need to get within twenty five yards to place the dart right in his torso. The tranquilizer should have him down within five minutes."

"That gives it five minutes to come after you." said Leo.

"Hopefully, I'll be able to sneak up behind it, and from a higher vantage point, place the dart in its back. If it tries to work its way up to where I hope to be, its own exertion will only speed up the chemical's path to its brain." replied Troy. "That sounds like a pretty good plan! You're the expert!" smiled Leo.

"That's why I've been on the cover of one magazine already!" boasted Troy. Leo shook his head and both men laughed at Troy's cockiness.

"Troy . . . I've been thinking about something . . ." paused Leo. "What is it?" asked Troy.

"I know that Ricky said we weren't to go after the creature without him, for safety reasons, but I want to capture this creature without the the interference of the Ricky or anyone else. I don't want to take a chance of having someone, with a gun, killing the poor thing. You and I need to go out there alone in order to bring it in alive. Are you with me on this?" asked Leo.

"Hey, that's fine with me. I'm sure we can do it. Hey, it's just a dumb animal right?" replied Troy.

"Let's hope so." replied Leo.

When do we go out there to get it?" asked Troy.

"How about tomorrow? Will you have time to get your equipment ready?" asked Leo.

"All I need is an hour. No problem." replied Troy.

"Then tomorrow we'll do it! . . . Uhhh . . . do you think we'd get in trouble for not following the orders of a law enforcement officer?" asked Leo.

"Hey, what's the worst thing that could happen to us? . . . A fine? A little jail time? So what!" It's worth it, Uncle Leo! smiled Troy.

"If we can bring in a live body, the ranger is not going to' complain, especially if it's that gray beast that attacked him. I just thought of something. I could arrange for us to have a helicopter take us out there!" smiled Troy.

"Helicopter? How much will that cost us?" asked Leo.

"Not a lot. I've got connections." winked Troy.

Chapter 13

Old Memories

Valentino's Sports Bar, considered the "hottest" club in the city of Lassiter, was overcrowded with customers. A news flash played across each of the large wall mounted television screens. The mood was normal as the customers watched the commercials that ran. Suddenly the news spokesman appeared with the news flash. "We interrupt this program as events are unfolding in the City of Lassiter. An alleged beast has terrorized a convenience store, and has reportedly abducted a customer. Our field report Katey Mooru is on scene with our first report." Katey Mooru quickly appeared on the television screen to deliver the limited information that they had. Customers at Valentino's Sports Bar sat in awe as they watched and listened to the reporter describe the alleged events that occurred at the Big Flower Convenience Store. "Can you believe this?" asked one older gentlemen to the bartender.

"I guess I can, since it's making statewide news!" he replied. "What do think the creature was?" asked the older gentlemen. "Don't know. Maybe it was that hairy ape everyone's been talking about all these years! Maybe it's real after all!" the bartender replied rather unconcernedly.

At a home in Denver a family was sitting on the sofa in front of the television. "Mommy, what kind of monster was that?" asked the seven-year-old boy. The mother just stared at the television is stark fear. At the University of Denver, students at a student lounge sat in disbelief as they listened to the news reporter. One of the students sarcastically remarked. "Oooooh, the monster ate him up. Now's he's coming to get some of you cuties in this dorm! Muahahahaha!" The other students looked at him, laughed, and shook their heads at one another heads.

The news reported then announced, "We'll be contacting the Lassiter County Sheriff's Department tonight for an official statement." Lt. Lincoln, of the Lassiter County Sheriff's Department, sat alone in the muster room watching the news.

"Oh, this is gonna be fun! Like I really want to talk with you!" he thought to himself. He walked to the door of the muster room and locked the door. He immediately got onto his computer to start up the word composing program so that he could begin an official statement for the media. Lt. Lincoln then called the desk officer to contact the deputies at the Big Flower Convenience Store to instruct them to call their updates in by cell phone, and thus avoid putting information out over their radios for the media to intercept. He also instructed the most junior deputy to bring a report to the station within as once he had obtained a sufficient amount of preliminary information.

One hour later, the news media arrived at the Sheriff's station seeking for "the one in charge" to get his public announcement. Lt. Lincoln had given numerous official statements, during the past few years. This was just another one he had to "act through" and try to look as convincing as he could. But this evening, he had an eerie feeling in his gut. He quickly tried to brush the feelings aside but discovered that he couldn't. The feelings of uneasiness came back and then began to grow and grow. It was a feeling he could not fully understand or explain. But, maybe he could. He thought to himself that maybe the reason for his uneasiness that one of his greatest curiosities or fears of his childhood may have just become a reality. He sat folded his arms and stared at the table in front of him. His mind went back to a time when he was an eleven year old boy.

The boy was walking along the snowy ridges with his .22 caliber rifle. He had been out for nearly an hour, yet had not yet been able to shoot a nice fat rabbit. He loved the sport. He loved his rifle. He loved the chasing rabbits. As he sat hidden behind the rocks, buried deep enough where he was sure nothing could see him. He spotted a nice fat cottontail rabbit in the distance. It was a little farther than what he was comfortable with, more than like too far for him to hit. No, he'd miss for sure. He had to get closer. Suddenly he noticed a smell. It was a rank odor that he never forgot all his life. *Where did it come from? How did that just come up out of nowhere?* He looked around to see if there was some carcass of some kind nearby. He turned around and there it was! Looking down into the ravine far below him he saw it. *Why is that big man carrying a like that?"* What a minute! That isn't a man! The thing was broader than anything that he ever saw, with massively shoulders, arms, torso, and legs. It had thick, shaggy, long hair. Its face was covered in hair. One thing was clearly distinguishable from that distance. It was those massive big bright white eyes and yellow irises. The beast was much bigger than any man, since it was maybe five times taller than the buck that it was carrying! It held the buck by the top of its neck and the top of it back. He could see blood on the body where the creature's claws sank into the dead buck. "Nobody can carry a heavy full grown buck like that!" he thought. The black shaggy creature continued on it carefree walk down the snowy ravine, oblivious to the fact that a boy was watching him. Not once did the creature look up in the direction of the boy. The creatures simply continued northward up the ravine as the boy watched it from above, from the west. The boy watched it for nearly fifteen minutes, until it disappeared behind the most northernmost ridge. It was gone. The boy quickly ran south, towards the highway, towards his bicycle, which he had pad-locked to an old rusty pole. He peddled home as quickly as he could, fearing that the creature, or one of its relatives, could be following him. He arrived at his front yard, and dropped the bike in the snow-covered grass. His friends were already in his front yard, throwing snowballs. There were a little surprised to see the panicked expression on the boy's face.

"I saw it! I saw it!" yelled the boy.

"You saw what?" asked one his friends.

"That big hairy monster that people told us about!" he replied. The boys all laughed him to scorn. The boy turn away from his friends, disappointed because their disbelief. He ran up the steps to his front door and ran inside, not closing the door. "Mom! Mom! I saw it!" he yelled, as he ran into the kitchen. His mother was pulling a dish pot out of the oven.

"What are talking about?" she asked.

"I saw that hairy snow creature that we heard stories about!" he exclaimed.

"Oh, really! Well, that's nice! Okay run along. I'm very busy right now!" she replied. She laughed and continued preparing lunch. The boy quickly ran outside to his friends again. As he came out of the front door, he was met by a barrage of snowballs. The boys through snowballs at him for several minutes, before they all ran away, laughing at him. Lincoln stood there on his porch watching the children run down the street. Would his friends believe his story? *Of course not!* He thought to himself. *Even Mom doesn't believe me!*

He sat on the patio chair for nearly fifteen minutes thinking about what he saw, earlier in the day. Finally it got to cold to sit any longer. He walked inside his house and up to his room. Was what he saw as an eleven year old boy one of those creatures?

Lt. Lincoln's thoughts came back to the present world. During the next hour he received numerous cell phone calls with information relating to the incident at the Big Flower Convenience Store. What was he going to tell the public? If he tells the news that an alleged creature was responsible for the attack, he will most likely forfeit his chance to be elected as Sheriff, within the next six months. If he tells the citizens it was a bear, he will be going against his own gut feelings that a monster is on the loose, and it may soon claim another victim.

How am I going to handle this? he thought to himself.

A deputy arrived, as ordered with preliminary reports of the incident scene. With the notes he compiled from the cell phone calls and the field report, he quickly compiled an official statement for the media. Within an hour, the reporters had arrived at the Sheriff's department. The media was invited into the Public Information Hall, where the American flag and the Sheriff's flag hung proudly before a royal blue curtained backdrop. Lt. Lincoln stood up straight and kingly in front of numerous cameras and lights. He stood up straight and tall and spoke firmly at the camera.

"Ladies and Gentlemen, as of yet, the Lassiter County Sheriff's Department has not confirmed the all the details regarding the attack that had taken place at the Big Flower Convenience Store. Our investigators are still busy interviewing people and analyzing facts and details. All we can say at this moment is that an unidentified man was abducted by an unidentified suspect. Our search teams are busy at this moment in an attempt to rescue the abducted individual. We will have more details later, as we obtain more facts. In the meantime, the Lassiter County Sheriff's Department advises you to please keep your children at home as soon as they are released from school. Citizens are prohibited from forming search parties or search parties relating to the incident of the Big Flower Convenience Store. This rule shall be enforced. Last of all, if you see anything suspicious, or anything that may be relevant to the case, please call the Lassiter County Sheriff's Department, immediately. Thank you for your time and attention!"

Lt. Lincoln quickly walked away from the camera stepped down from the platform. That's about as politically correct I can be, for now! He thought as he tried to outrun the reporters. "Lieutenant, was the victim taken by a monster?" yelled a reporter.

"Lieutenant, what kind of creature had taken the victim?" shouted another reporter.

"Is it true that large footprints were discovered at the scene of the incident?" shouted a third reporter. Ignoring the reporters Lt. Lincoln continued to quickly walk out of the Public Information Hall.

"Good statement, Sir!" remarked a deputy who was walking beside Lincoln.

"Short and concise! The less the media and the public knows, the better!" replied Lt. Lincoln.

Chapter 14

Helicopter

The blue helicopter flew effortlessly through the majestic Colorado Rocky Mountains. Behind the controls was Rudy Bankings, a well-tattooed, long haired hippie, who had a passion for flying, as much as he had a passion for playing the electric guitar. Rudy played in a rock n' roll band prior to obtaining his helicopter pilot license. Troy, was the drummer! Together they toured the south for nearly five years before the band disbanded, and each member went their separate ways. Rudy and Troy were the best friends, since middle school, and could nearly read each other's mind. Rudy had been so financially successful during the past few years that money was unimportant. This ride provided to Troy was free. He would do anything for his best friend.

"Dude, now what are we hunting for?" asked Rudy.

"I told you already. A big hairy monster." smiled Troy.

"Yeah, whatever! I can't believe I let you talk me into this! You gonna' owe me a lot of beer for this!" laughed Rudy.

"You'll get as much as you want!" laughed Troy. Troy placed his finger on the map.

"This is the place that the hunters told us that they heard the creature and spotted its tracks." said Troy.

"I've only been there once or twice, maybe a year ago. It's a treacherous area, but I think I can fly you in there." replied the Rudy.

After a twenty minute flight, Rudy announced, "Troy, we are at the GPS coordinates the hunters gave you."

"Okay." replied Troy, as he surveyed the area through his binoculars.

Rudy brought the helicopter to a hover just eleven feet off of the ground. Troy looked out of the passenger window for the creature. All he could see was torrents of snow swirling all around him, whipped up by the helicopters rotor.

"I know he's around here! I can just feel it! This was the last area that the hunters spotted it! If it's not here, at least we should still be able to see its tracks."

Troy had difficulty seeing through the heavy snow that was falling.

"Visibility is not too good!" said Rudy.

"Yeah, it's pretty bad!" agreed Troy.

"Look, there's the truck under that large tree!"

"Where, I can't see it?" asked Rudy.

"Look a little more to your eleven o'clock." replied Troy.

"Okay, got it. I see it!" replied Rudy.

"Can you land?" asked Troy.

"Sure!" replied Rudy.

The helicopter came to rest in a clearing, just a few meters from the truck. As the two men searched the area, they were disappointed to discover that there were no footprints or any tracks to be found.

"A lot of snow fell, within the couple of hours. If there were footprints, they're probably completely filled in!" announced Troy. The men trudged around in nearly knee-deep snow for nearly thirty minutes. The snow appeared to be getting higher with each minute.

"Can we fly a few circles around the area to see if we can spot any movement." asked Troy.

"Sure, but only for a little while, I have to keep an eye on our fuel supply." replied Rudy.

"Yeah, I understand." replied Troy.

Rudy hovered slowly along the ground, at an altitude of only eleven feet for nearly ten minutes, when suddenly and unexpectedly the creature reached up and grabbed the left skid of the helicopter, below Rudy's seat. The creature began to violently pull the helicopter downward until it could look into Rudy's window. It roared into Rudy's window. Rudy looked in horror at the creature massively wide, fanged mouth. He immediately tried to pull the helicopter into a vertical climb but the creature's downward pull caused the helicopter to veer out of control. The creature released its grip forcing Rudy to overcompensate with the flight controls. The helicopter shot upwards at an angle but pitched and rolled in every direction as Rudy fought to bring the vehicle under control. Immediately the helicopter went into a flat tailspin.

"Hang on!" screamed Rudy. Feelings of terror and hopelessness filled both men as the helicopter continued mercilessly on its seemingly endless tailspin. Rudy frantically continued to try to regain control of the vehicle as his rotor sliced into the trees on the passenger's side. Large pieces of rotor fragments flew in every direction and large branches pierced the helicopter's windows as it the vehicle's fuselage slammed into the dense trees. The vehicle immediately dropped straight downward and crashed on top of the snow-covered boulders. Within seconds, what remained of the main rotor stopped spinning and the engine went silent. Both Rudy and Troy looked at each other. The force of the landing bent both skids and the boulders punctured the bottom of the fuselage. The cabin was filled with branches, leaves, broken glass, a torn wiring harness, and snow. All windows were shattered.

"Are you okay?" asked Rudy. Troy looked at his own arms and legs.

"I don't see anything wrong on me, but you don't look so good!" replied Troy.

"What do you mean by that?" asked Rudy. Rudy looked down and noticed that a shard of steel had entered the back of his right thigh, and was protruding nearly three inches out of the top of his thigh.

"I think it missed the femoral artery." said Rudy dryly.

"How bad does it hurt?" asked Troy.

"More than I want to show." winced Rudy. Rudy attempted to key the radio's microphone.

"The microphone is dead." said Rudy.

"I'll use my cell . . . oh no!" said Troy, as he fumbled through his jacket and looked around the seat. He then realized it was in his hand when the creature grabbed the skid.

It's in my bag, behind the seat." replied Rudy. Troy looked behind Rudy seat, only to be dismayed to see a gaping hole where there aircraft sheet metal used to be.

Both men looked at each other in stark surprise. They were perhaps twenty miles from the nearest highway or any place where they find help.

"Dude, you're going owe me more than just beer for this mess!" said Rudy.

"Yeah, man!" laughed Troy. Suddenly they heard the angry wail of the creature of which they had temporarily forgotten about.

"Oh no!" said Rudy. Both men began to tremble.

"Unbuckle the seat belts! Troy, get your gun!" shouted Rudy desperately.

"It's behind me!" replied Troy. Troy and Rudy were both able to quickly unbuckle their seatbelts. Rudy reached behind Troy's seat and grabbed the rifle. The force of the crash rammed the rifle's barrel through the vehicles aluminum floor.

Rudy pulled frantically, but had to stop due the pain in his right leg.

"Aaaaaack! You pull it!" screamed Rudy, as the pain in his leg intensified. Troy jumped out of the shattered door, reached behind his seat, and began to pull on the rifle. After a long two, Troy was finally able to rip the rifle out of the floor panel, but to his disappointment, discovered that the tranquilizer rifle's barrel was bent beyond use.

"Do you have a real gun?" asked Rudy.

"No." replied Troy.

"Smart!" replied Rudy sarcastically. The creature let out another angry wail.

"It's getting closer!" yelled Troy. Frantically the men looked around them in all directions but only saw thick branches, snow, boulders, and trees. They could smell the creature, whose stench was getting stronger with each passing second. "It's coming! Grab something, anything long and sharp!" yelled Troy.

"Aaaaack! Help me!" screamed Rudy, pointing the shard that was sticky out of his thigh. The men quickly looked around the cabin for anything that could be used as a weapon. As Rudy turned in his seat he shrieked in pain. The metal shard that was protruding out of the top of his right thigh sliced more and more of his quadriceps, with each of his movement. Suddenly the creature appeared about ten feet in front. The men tremble in horror as the creature walked up to the front of the helicopter. The creature thrusted out its massive, shaggy arms at the men's heads, but met resistance against the cockpit's canopy. The creature slowly walked to Rudy's side and looked into the window at Rudy. Rudy, filled with horror, trembled violent as he looked into the bizarre, angry face of the beast. The creature ripped the door off of its hinges, reached, it shaggy arm in, and grabbed Rudy by his chest and tried to forcefully pull him from the vehicle. The seatbelt, however, kept Rudy secured to the seat. Rudy screamed out in terror and in pain as the metal shard continued to slice into his leg, with each of the creature's pulled. Instinctively, Troy reached over and grabbed Rudy by the right arm, trying to keep the creature from pulling his friend out of the vehicle. The merciless tug of the creature lasted for several seconds, with Rudy screaming out in pain and terror. Troy frantically looked around for anything he could use as a weapon when he discovered shattered glass behind him. He reached over to his right side and picked up an eleven inch shard of the passenger window and jabbed it repeatedly into the creature's clawed hand. The shard cut Troy's palm with each jab into the creature's arm. Troy screamed out in terror and fury as he repeatedly stabbed the massive gray hand. After the tenth stab, the creature finally released is furious grip. The creature wailed and then drew back its arm and backed away from the helicopter with the shard still lodged in the back of its claw. The creature pulled the shard out of its hand, roared, and stepped back towards the helicopter and looked inside. The men were gone! Troy had quickly unbuckled Rudy and pulled him out of the seat. Both men fled through the passenger side door. Troy placed Rudy's left arm over his own shoulder, and both men ran down the ravine. The creature walked to the passenger side to discover both men nearly fifty yards away. The creature quickly gave chase.

"Hurry, Hurry!" screamed Troy. Rudy cried out for pain repeated with as they ran. Each step sent waves of sharp pain throughout Rudy's entire being. The metal shard had completely sliced through his outer quadriceps. Although the shard missed his femoral artery, the right pant was soaked with blood. The men made their way towards a fast moving Powakana River. The river was nearly twenty-five yards across, only a few feet deep, and flowed extremely fast. The creature was quickly gaining on the men. The men painfully made their way over the snow covered rocks that lined the shore of the river. Halfway through the rocks, Troy's foot landed on an unstable rock, which turned, causing both men to fall sideways. A sharp pain shot up through Troy's leg. The sprain on his ankle caused Troy to cry out in pain.

"Get up! Get up!" screamed Troy. The men struggled to their feet as they continued make their way towards the water. As they looked behind them they discovered the creature had already made it to the edge of the rocks and was closing in on them. Just was the men reached the water's edge, the creature's claws sank deep into Troy's left shoulder. The four inched claws sank deep into his flesh causing Troy to scream out in pain and terror. Troy instinctively pushed Rudy into the fast moving river. Rudy plunged headfirst into the icy currents. The icy cold water felt like an electrical shock causing his body to stiffen like a rigid board. He saw the round smooth stones on the river bottom rushing under him as the fast current mercilessly pulled him downstream. He felt the smooth rocks hit his back as he was being pulled along by the current. As he was tossed and turned underwater, he found himself looking up towards the surface of the fast moving water. While chocking on water, he frantically tried to position himself in a sitting position then gave a massive kick on the river bed to launch himself upwards. He broke the surface of the water and gasped for air. He looked and saw the creature many yards upstream, feasting on its latest victim.

Chapter 15

The Indians and the Creatures

Nearly four days after the attack occurred at the Big Flower Convenience Store, the Sheriff's squad car dropped off Julie Blackhawk at the gate of the Yemanache Indian Reservation. A Bureau of Indian Affairs police officer then placed Julie in his own squad car and took Julie to her house, where her mother was waiting anxiously for her. Julie ran up the dirt path and up the stairs to the front door. She fell into her mother's arms and wept. Her mother quickly closed the door and escorted Julie to her room.

"I never thought that I would see it happen in my lifetime." whispered Julie.

"Neither did I." replied her mother.

"Mom, I thought there was some kind of understanding between us and them." said Julie.

"Me too. I don't know what happened." replied her mother somberly.

Within minutes, Julie was sound asleep.

Two days later, a deputy and a Bureau of Indian Affairs police officer stood at Julie's doorstep.

"Miss Julie Anderson?" asked Deputy Mills.

"Yes. Come in." she replied. The men sat down with Julie and her mother at the kitchen table. Deputy Mills was alarmed to see how different Julie looked today. One the night of the attack, her eyes were red with tears, her hair was a mess, and she was in emotional meltdown. Today, she looked calm and strikingly beautiful. When Julie looked up to see Mills staring at her lips, Mills quickly looked away and blushed.

We wanted to know if there were any more details that you could give us that could help us in our investigation." said Mills.

"Okay." whispered Julie.

"Do I have your consent to record this interview on my voice recorder?" asked Mills.

"Okay." replied Julie, nodding her head up and down.

"I think my mother should tell you what she knows." said Julie. Julie's mother looked down at the table and sat quietly for a moment, as if she did not want to talk.

"Mother, please tell them!" pleaded Julie. Her mother reluctantly looked at the two officers. After a moment, she finally spoke.

"It wasn't a man visited the store." said Julie's mother. She sat quietly again for a brief moment.

"Okay, . . . and what else?" asked deputy Mills.

"It was a Laminiki." said Julie's mother gravely.

"Could you write that word down for me?" asked Deputy Mills. Deputy Mills handed her a small note pad and watched her as she wrote down the name.

"Can you explain to me what you are talking about?" asked Mills.

"They are the keepers of the mountains. Our forefather knew of them. Our people have always known of them. Their first encounter with them, generations ago, was not a good one." said Julie's mother.

"Why was it not a good one?" asked Mills.

"Generations ago, some of our leader were out hunting for buffalo. They reached the top of a mountain and looked down into the valley below them. They saw what they thought was the back of a small man, attacking a buffalo, far below them. They thought that it was a person from another tribe, who had crossed into our lands to steal our buffalo. The hunters quietly and made their way down to meet the intruder and kill him. When the hunters came up behind him, the man turned around. The hunters then realized that the intruder was not a man. They drew out their arrows and killed the beast. As it lay dying on the ground in front of them, they heard the roar of some unknown animal. The hunters looked up to see another beast of the same kind quickly came down the mountain towards them. It was twice as tall as the one that they killed. They fought against the oncoming beast, but it killed all of the hunters, except one, my great grandfather. He was able to escape and run back to the camp.

"The two creatures were the Lamaniki." The eyes of both Mills and the Indian police officer were fixed on Julie's mother. The manner of which Julies mother told the story literal took Mills back in time with her. It was so eerie that Mills could see in his mind the actual event, as if he was actually there. It was mystical and downright scary. Mills shivered as he heard the story, although the room was warm.

"My grandfather drew pictures of the beast, using ashes from a campfire. It has been kept in our family library for all these years." said Julie's mother.

"Can you show me the pictures?" asked Mills. Julie's mother sat quietly and looked away.

"Mother, show them!" pleaded Julie. Julies mother walked over to the bookshelf and pulled out a old photo album and brought it to the table. The old leather photo album was cracked at the edges. Mills looked at the old album and was amazed it didn't fall apart while Julie's mother pried it open. Within the old were numerous pictures of Native Americans, in tribal dress, in various, somber poses.

"Your people don't smile when photographed?" asked Mills. Julie and her mother looked at him, without answering his question. On the last page of the photo album, Julie's mother found what she was looking for, a closed, but unsealed envelope, nearly as large as the photo album itself. She opened the old envelope and pull out the pictures.

Everyone at the table looked inside to see what old drawings, which had been kept inside for all these years. Mills and the Indian police officer sat in awe as the handed the hand-drawn pictures of the beast. It was exactly like the ones that Ricky Toomis had drawn!

"Ma'am, may I please make copies of these drawings? I promise that I will take good care of them and return them to you, no later than tomorrow." asked Mills.

"That will be fine." replied Julie's mother.

"Is there anything more that you could tell us?" asked Mills.

"No." replied Julie's mother."

"Julie?" asked Mills.

"No." she replied.

"Ladies thank you for your time and cooperation. We'll come tomorrow with these drawings." said Mills. The two officers left. They slowly drove back to the reservation's security office.

"I can't believe what I've got in my hands. All this time I thought that Ranger was out of his mind. Delerious." said Mills. The Indian police officer acted as if he didn't hear Mills, but instead continued to drive towards the front gate." After a few seconds the Indian police officer spoke. "In the past, I regarded the Lamaniki as nothing more than just a legend. Now, I keep my gun under my bed at night, in case they come for me." replied the Indian officer.

"Why would they come for you?" asked Mills.

"I don't know. I can't explain it. I just have this feeling that something bad is going to happen to us, here at the reservation.

"Really? How long have you had this feeling?" asked Mills. "Since we heard of the attack at Sampson River Road." replied the officer.

Julie and her mother sat quietly at the table.

"Why are they attacking man now?" asked Julie..

"I don't know." she replied.

"Mother, will the attacks continue?" asked Julie

"I don't know." she replied.

Chapter 16

The Truck

In spite of the warning given by Lt. Lincoln, numerous small groups of hunters immediately began organizing teams to hunt down and kill the alleged "hairy monster" of the Rocky Mountains. Among them were two hunters, Old Jerry and a young man named Kyle. The next morning, these two hunters were walking through a region only five miles north of the Big Flower Convenience store. The Sheriff's department posted nearly one hundred signs, across the county, prohibiting search parties and hunting parties regarding the incident. The two hunters ignored the warnings posted along the highway. They had entered the heavily ridge area through a remote and seldom used area. They were both carrying .308 rifles and were determined to find this "supposed monster" or at least capture some video footage of it. An encounter with this monster was a chance of a lifetime for them and it was more than they could resist. After all, *"What was the most that law enforcement could do them? Give them a fine, or maybe a few days in jail? Who cares? Any video they could obtain should bring them some degree of fame or fortune. It was worth it the risk!* They reasoned. The hunters climbed to the top of five hundred feet tall ridge and found a highpoint with huge boulders.

"We can conceal ourselves behind these rocks, kiddo!" said Old Jerry. Both men sat hidden and peered through their binoculars for nearly four hours.

"Can we go home now?" asked Kyle.

"We're not gonna spot nothing!" he thought to himself. "Patience, my boy! Don't you want to be on some talk show, in front of millions, with you video of that hairy ape?" asked Old Jerry.

Bingo, their wish came through! Old Jerry spotted the creature, topping out onto a southwestern ridge, nearly a mile away. It was walking in their direction, unaware of the men's presence.

"Is that a black bear?" asked Old Jerry. Kyle peered curiously through his own binoculars, trying to see if were actually a bear. Minutes passed. The black figure continued northward towards them.

"Oh my! That's not a black bear!" gasped Old Jerry.

"Black bears don't walk for that long of a distance on two feet!" shrieked the Kyle.

"Kid, write down our GPS coordinates, quickly!" whispered Old Jerry. The young man pulled out his GPS, pen, and small memo book from his parka.

"Okay, I got them!" the young man whispered.

"He should be close enough to video now, give me the video recorder!" whispered Old Jerry. The young man reached into his back pack and pulled the DVD recorder out and handed it to Old Jerry. Old Jerry began shooting the video on the black figure. The figure about one half of a mile away, but it was clearly walking on two legs, something that bears don't do for very long. The creature's broad shoulders caused it to vaguely resemble a man in pitch black football gear. "It's big, really big!" laughed Old Jerry. Kyle viewed the creature through binoculars in wide-eyed astonishment.

"I can't believe it. Look at the size of that thing." The Kyle stood up to stretch his legs, while still peering through is binoculars.

"Get down kid! Do you want it to spot us?" barked the barked Old Jerry. Kyle quickly dropped low. But it was too late. The quick movement of the Kyle caught the creature's eye.

The creature stopped and looked at the ridge towards its northeast. It knew it was food. Nearly a minute passed. The creature suddenly entered a running gate, down into the drawn that separated the creature and the men.

"It running . . . towards us!" gasped Old Jerry. Fear gripped both men. Their hope of shooting or videoing the creature, unawares, was swept away.

"Did it see us?" asked Kyle.

"Us?" barked the Old Jerry. "It saw you!" The creature reached the bottom of the drawn, just south of the men and began it's climb up the ridge.

"It's coming up to us!" said Old Jerry was he continued to video the creature. Kyle continued to watch the creature through his binoculars. He was able to see the creature's teeth and clawed grey hands. Old Jerry quickly turned off the video recorder and jammed it into his parka. He grabbed his rifle, and quickly ran, leaving Kyle behind him. Kyle looked at the man run, and then looked down the ridge to see the creature quickly approaching. Kyle also grabbed his own rifle and ran after Old Jerry. For nearly four minutes, both men ran down the ridge towards their truck. Kyle stopped to catch his breath.

He looked up the ridge behind him to see that the creature topping out on the ridge. He then turned and continued to run down the snowy winding ridge. Old Jerry reached the truck, gasping for breath. He opened the truck and through his backpack in. He pointed his rifle up the ridge toward the black figure. He pulled the bolt to chamber a round. "Hurry up!" he yelled towards Kyle. Kyle continued to run down the ridge. He reached a steep rock waterfall, a little over one hundred yards from the truck. Kyle threw his backpack over the rock waterfall and then slung the rifle over his back. He then began a steep climb down the rock waterfall. Halfway down, his foot hit a flat, slick, ice covered rock. His foot slipped, causing the young man to tumble down the rest of the waterfall. The fall was so violent that it broke one of the young man's ribs. The young man's rifle fell and tumbled down the waterfall. Kyle cried out in agony. The creature also suddenly reached top of the waterfall. Old Jerry, standing behind the driver's door, was able to place his front sight on the creature. His fear was so intense that his entire body trembled. He pulled trigger. The shot missed the creature. He pulled the bolt to chamber another round. He frantically tried to take aim and fired again. He missed. He chambered a third round, took aim and fired. This time, the round hit the creature in the shoulder. The force of the round knocked the creature against the rocks. It regained its footing and continued its descent. Kyle lying prostrate in the snow, scrambled to his feet, and ran towards the truck, limping and holding his ribs. Old Jerry chambered another round and took aim. Kyle reached the passenger door just as Old Jerry pulled the trigger. The shot missed. The creature made it the bottom of the rocky waterfall and made its way swiftly towards the truck, with its arms outstretch, as if ready to grab anything within reach. It let out a hauntingly unusual roar, unlike anything the men had ever heard before. Old Jerry quickly started the motor and placed the vehicle in reverse to increase the distance between them and the oncoming creature. He turned the vehicle quickly to the right when suddenly the rear two tires dropped into a deep ditch.

The bottom of the truck bottomed out and the rear tires hung over edge and spun wildly.

"Put it in four wheels!" yelled Kyle.

"It's only a two-wheel drive truck!" replied Old Jerry. They looked up to see the creature only a few feet away. Old Jerry reached behind him to grab the rifle. The creature immediate came to the driver's door and ripped the door completely off its hinges. It grabbed Old Jerry by his left arm and pulled him out of the truck. It began to swing its helpless victim wildly until the arm dislocated and ripped out of its socket. The man's body was thrown several yards away from the truck. The creature then tried to reach for the Kyle in the passenger side. Kyle opened the passenger door and fell backwards out of the truck. He immediately scrambled underneath the truck for cover. The creature, looking into the driver door and no longer seeing the second man, then turned around to see the man that was thrown from the vehicle. Old Jerry had already gone into shock. The creature began feasting on the unconscious victim. Kyle under the truck scrambled out and made a frantic run towards the highway, which was only about five hundred meters away. Once he made it to the highway he flagged down a car and immediately placed a called to 911.

Within thirty minutes, four sheriff's vehicles and a two U.S. Forest Rangers arrived to the site of the attack. News Channel 7 and News Channel 9 arrived shortly afterwards.

"Oh no! Our little secret is no longer a secret." said Ricky dryly, over his cell phone, to Deputy Mills, as he saw news cameramen and reporters beginning their live broadcasts. The deputies arrived to the site of the attack. They found the truck, hanging helpless over the deep ditch, a severed arm, and a massive blood stained away only ten yards away. There was no body or any other remains.

"Officers look!" shouted a news reporter. The deputies and rangers ran to see what the news reporter wanted to show them. There in the snow, large, eighteen inch footprints and drops of blood, led northward, towards the high snow-capped ridges. The deputies and the two rangers began the chase.

Chapter 17

Troy Bellingmay

At 7:05 a.m., Ricky sat at his home computer checking his personal emails, reviewing the local news, and sports headlines. He didn't notice anything rather exciting, other than that the fact that the Denver Broncos were doing well this season, in comparison to last year's losing streak. *That's a nice change*! he smiled. His cell phone rang.

"Hello?" answered Ricky.

"Good, good morning Ricky, this is Professor Leo Kluud! Do you remember me?" laughed Dr. Kluud enthusiastically.

"Oh . . . how could I forget, Leo! What can I do for you?" Ricky politely replied.

"Ricky, I would like to know if I could meet with you sometime this week, at your office. Remember that I told you earlier that I had a plan? We'll I want to explain it in greater detail. I want to introduce to you a young man, who is part of that plan." said the Leo.

"Okay . . . well I am heading to my office now and I'll be there for about an hour . . . I could meet you then. How does that sound?" replied Ricky.

"Splendid! We'll come now!" Leo gleefully replied. "Okay . . . see you then!" replied Ricky.

"Okay, bye then!" Leo hanged up.

This plan better be good! Ricky asked himself as he shook his head. At the office, Ricky was busy reviewing the narrative he had written regarding the creature that attacked him. He put more effort in this report than any report he had ever written in the past.

"Officer Toomis, Dr. Kluud and Troy Bellingmay are here to see you!" said Anne, the records technician.

"Send them in please!" replied Ricky. Ricky looked up from the front desk of the Ranger station to see a smiling Professor Kluud and a long-haired young man, perhaps in his mid twenties walking into his office. Ricky stood up and greeted them with a firm and friendly handshake. The young man appeared to be very lean, goateed, and wearing a very modern-looking, woodland camouflage hunting coat. The young man's hair was nearly down to his waist, in a long, single black pony tail. He was also a funky-looking tattoo half buried under his collar, on the left side of his neck. He had two obtrusive earrings too.

Ricky, was not impressed. *Okay, so in which pocket was he keeping the weed?* Ricky thought to himself.

"Good, good morning, Ricky! I would to introduce to you, Mr. Troy Bellingmay." Dr. Kluud said proudly.

Troy Bellingmay? Hmmm, I think I know that name! No way! It can't be the same person . . . thought Ricky.

"Good morning, Troy!" said Ricky.

"Good morning, Mr. Toomis!" Troy answered politely. "Gentlemen can I offer you some coffee?" asked Ricky.

"Yes, please, black with no sugar." replied Professor Kluud, as he took off his red scarf.

"Nothing for me, thanks." replied Troy.

"Hey, tell me about those Broncos!" laughed Ricky.

"They on a roll!" laughed Troy.

"Indeed they are!" laughed Dr. Kluud.

After a few minutes of football talk, the men got down to business.

"Are you Troy Bellingmay, the safari hunter?" asked Ricky, politely, but directly.

"That'd be me!" Troy replied proudly.

"I read and article about you and saw your picture, next to that African elephant, in some hunting magazine last year. That article describing how you brought it down with one shot, from two hundred yards was interesting!" said Ricky.

"Thank you!" smiled Troy.

"Troy, how old are you?" Ricky asked.

"Twenty-five." replied Troy.

"How long have you been a hunter?" asked Ricky.

"Since I was fifteen." smiled Troy.

"Long time!" replied Ricky.

"Leo how did you get a hold of Troy?" asked Ricky

"Well . . . uh hmm . . . he's my nephew." replied Leo.

"Your nephew? Well, aren't you full of surprises!" laughed Ricky.

"It is true!" replied Leo proudly.

"Oh . . . I get it. You want me to give you permission for Troy to shoot the creature that attacked me!" said Ricky.

"Yes, but to tranquilize it, not to kill it" replied Leo, lifting his index finger for emphasis."Ha ha ha!" Ricky laughed.

"Troy have you ever tranquilized a big animal before?" asked Ricky.

"Twice." affirmed Troy.

"We'll, I guess that better than none at all!" laughed Ricky. The three men laughed together.

"Ricky, when you are fully healed, please allow us to go with you to find the creature.

Looking at Ricky, Leo could tell that Ricky was obviously not too thrilled about the idea.

"Troy, how much is he paying you for this?" asked Ricky.

"He's not!" replied Troy.

After a brief pause and moment of quiet thinking, Ricky spoke.

"Troy, could you please tell me a little bit about yourself?"

"Yes Sir! I graduated from the University of Iowa with a degree in Liberal Arts, worked for my dad in his construction company, and do a lot of hunting in my spare time!" replied Troy, excitedly.

"So your dad owns a construction company?" asked Ricky.

"Yep!" replied Troy proudly.

"Good! Ummm . . . . can you tell me something about your hunting experiences?"

"Well I got a few antlers hanging up in my living room, but most of all, I did go on a hunting trip in Africa, last year." replied Troy.

"And you got an elephant!" asked Ricky.

"Yep, I shot her with a tranquilizer for the Kenyan government. I rode along with their team, as an extra hand, but I was actually the lucky one that landed the shot. It really upset their own rangers to have some American dude make the shot, when their own government workers hit the animal!"

"Why couldn't they?" asked Ricky.

"They missed, I didn't! They found the elephant with one pink tranquilizer dart in it. I was the only shooter that had pink darts. They were really jealous!" replied Troy with a huge smile on his face.

Ricky lifted his eyebrows in surprise.

"Oh! I guess I'd be jealous too!" laughed Ricky.

After another brief pause Ricky spoke.

"Troy would you please wait outside for just a moment?" Ricky politely asked.

"Yes, sir!" replied Troy.

As soon as Troy closed the door, Ricky spoke.

"I'm sorry Leo, he is not coming with us."

"What? Why?" asked Professor Kluud.

"Leo, did you tell him what we are after?" asked Ricky.

"Yes, I did!" replied Dr. Kluud.

"Well I appreciate your honesty but Troy isn't going with us. Leo, with all due respect, I was in the process of having one of my own rangers go with me to shoot the creature. I didn't know that your plan was to get a shooter from the outside. especially a renown hunter like Troy. I wanted to keep the circle of involvement as limited as possible. The U.S. Forest Service, for the time being, will only give limited information to the media and to the public, as we deem necessary. We don't want to cause a panic, or cause monster hunting parties to start forming. Our Service, with local law enforcement will to handle this matter, alone. Troy, may have his own webpage or be part of some social networking website. We don't want him posting information regarding the creature." explained Ricky.

Dr. Kluud sat calmly and just looked at Ricky.

"I am sorry Leo but let law enforcement handle the matter."

"Okay. Ricky if you change you mind and you want Troy to tranquilize the creature, would you please call me?" asked Leo.

"If I change my mind, I will call you." replied Ricky. "Leo, I really need to go. I do want to thank for your time and your enthusiasm to help the Service regarding this matter." said Ricky.

"Thank you for your time!" replied Leo with a hint of disappointment.

Ricky and Leo stepped out into the hallway where Troy was waiting.

"Troy it was a pleasure to meet you! Good luck on your future hunts! I hope to see you with another elephant or something big in next year's magazine!" smiled Ricky.

"Thank you!" smiled Troy.

Dr. Kluud and Troy left quietly.

"Officer Toomis, what did they want?" asked Anne, the records technician.

"Ohhh . . . they just wanted to know if I was doing better. I told them that I was healing well!" smiled Ricky.

Chapter 18

Recreational Vehicle

Daryl McLeek, drove his new recreation vehicle cautiously up the steep two-lane road towards the peak. His wife Maggie sat asleep, in the passenger's seat, with Bailey asleep on her lap. The light snowfall made driving conditions a little more difficult. The speed limited was 45, but due to weather conditions, and the size of the RV, he thought it would be better to drive at about 25 miles per hour. Fortunately, his vehicle was the only vehicle on the road. They had traveled from Nevada to enjoy skiing at the newly opened ski resort, King's Castle. Daryl and Maggie had already visited the Winter Park Ski Resort, but King's Castle was supposedly "bigger and better." The King's Castle Ski Resort had an impressive motel, built to resemble a, German-style castle. This was the opening week of the new resort, and expectations were high. The resort also boasted the best skiing slopes in the state. It was a vacation that the McLeek and his wife had been planning for, since his promotion at the insurance company he worked for.

Daryl stopped at an empty rest area, halfway up the steep mountain. They parked at the further point from the restroom, at the area overlooking the majesty range of the Rocky Mountains.

"Daryl, I'm going to Bailey for a walk!" announce Maggie, his wife.

"Okay, don't go too far, it's getting cold out there!" he replied from the RV's shower. Maggie opened the door of the RV and Bailey jumped out. The old Yorkshire terrier sank up to his belly in the fresh snow. Maggie, zipping up her coat, gingerly step down, and tested the depth of the fresh snow. Maggie felt the wind push her along as she walked away from the RV, as she followed Bailey. Bailey continued to walk through the trees, along a flat area of grass. The path was not a walkway, but easy enough for the both the dog and Maggie to traverse. Maggie looked around her in wonder.

"So beautiful!" she thought to herself. The afternoon sky was brightly overcast, the snow was quite heavy. In the past she could only image what the Colorado Rockies would look like. Today, she saw firsthand, that the Rockies was truly the most beautiful place in the world. The wind blew strongly against Maggie's back, but she didn't mind. Her new coat, gloves, and wool hat, kept her nice and warm. Bailey appeared to be doing fine. Maggie pulled out her camera and began to take pictures of the area snowy peaks. Before she knew it, nearly fifteen minutes had past. She took nearly thirty pictures of the trees, Bailey, and the incredible horizon. Maggie looked behind her and noticed that she was much farther from the rest area than she thought she would. Suddenly a fear overcame her.

Bears! There are bears up here in Colorado, right? She thought to herself.

"Bailey! Bailey!" she shouted. The dog turned and perked his ears up, looking at her. The wind continued to push against Maggies back and blew away from the dog. For that reason, Bailey could not smell what was hiding in front of him. The creature was tucked in, behind a thick patch of snow-covered pines. It peered between the branches, and was as still as the boulders around it. The creature watched the dog intensely, hoping it would get closer and closer. The snow covered branches were so thick, and the creature was so still, no one would have noticed its presence. That is how it survived all these centuries. It watched as the unsuspecting dog and human approached it. It just stood there and waited, slightly crouched, with its arms outstretched, instinctively ready to rush in for the kill. It looked at the dog. It looked at the woman, trying to decide which one to grab. It decided to go for larger of the two. Maggie's cellular phone rang out with her customary Bee Gee's ringtone.

"Maggie, where are you?" asked Daryl.

"Oh, I'm not far. I am still in sight of RV. Bailey's just doing his thing out here in the snow. We're on our way back . . . . Aaaaarghhhhh!" she screamed.

"Maggie! Maggie! Maggie what's happening!" screamed Daryl. Maggie looked up to see the branches get pushed aside and the massive beast rushed out with its arms outstretched in the direction of the woman. Maggie dropped the cellular telephone in the snow and ran forward, towards the beast, in an effort to grab Bailey. Bailey, upon seeing the creature, instinctively attacked. The dog fearlessly ran up to the oncoming monster and leaped at its leg. The dog latched onto the leg of creature and sank its teeth into the flesh as far as it could. The creature let out mountain-shaking wail and reached frantically for the dog.

"Bailey!" screamed Maggie. Maggie turned and ran. She ran a few steps when she logged her foot in between two large rocks. The forward momentum of her running pressed her shin against the rock causing her shin bone to snap. Her forward momentum sent her flying to the snowing path. She hit the ground, screaming in pain. Maggie rolled over onto her back and saw the creature quickly approaching her, holding the dead dog in its massive hand. Maggie screamed in horror as she tried to pull herself backwards through the snow. Within seconds he huge creature nearly on top of her when she felt the arms reach under and around her. Daryl pulled her backwards, supported her torso, and the back of her knees. He scooped her up out of the snow and ran as fast as he possible could. As Daryl ran, he turned to look at the creature, walking closely behind him. He reached the RV climbed up the steps and laid Maggie on the floor, turned and ran back to close the side door. As soon he latched the door and set the lock, creature's hands had slammed against the vehicle. The creature grabbed the passenger side mirror and the top of the RV and began to shake the RV violently. The shaking tossed the man and his injured wife, from side to side. Maggie screamed out each time she was slammed against the sides of the RV. The man fought desperately to get to his feet, as the creature continued to pull and shake the vehicle. Somehow Daryl was able to climb over Maggie, while they were being thrown from side-to-side. He reached under her arms and pulled her backwards toward the rear of the RV, as far from the side door as possible. He stumbled back to the center of the RV and reached over the sink and yanked open the overhead kitchen cabinet. A .38 caliber revolver flew out and landed in the sink. Suddenly the entrance door to the RV was ripped off of its hinges and the creature reached its massive clawed hand inside and proceeded to grab at anything it could. The creature latched onto Daryl's shoe and squeezed onto his foot. Daryl, let out a scream as he felt the crushing force on his foot. He instinctively jerked his leg away. His foot slipped out the shoe, but the claws of the creature sliced into the sides of his foot. Daryl scrambled backwards toward the rear of the vehicle. The creature was able to put its head inside but was unable to squeeze it massive shoulders in. It looked it at the terrified occupant and let out a nightmarish wail. The woman and the man screamed in terror as they looked into the huge, hiedeous face of the attacking beast. Dary reached frantically to grab the wet revolver. He was able to grab the gun take aim. He fired two rounds at the hand that was reaching for them, but missed as the creature violently shook the RV from side-to-side.

"Someone is shooting a gun!" screamed the old man's wife, from inside the restroom.

People near the restroom, stood terrified, not knowing from which direction the gunfire came from. Other people, not knowing why, watched the RV shaking violently, side to side. A curious old man made his way towards the RV. As he got closer he was able to see the creature frantically try to squeeze inside the vehicle. The old man turned and ran. The people in the restroom, ran to their cars, and quickly left the rest area, fearing the sound of gunfire.

"Call the police! Call the police!" he yelled in his old weak voice, as he hobbled back to the restroom to find his wife. Daryl was able to take hold of the gun that was knocked from his hand. He took aim at the groping hand and fire two more rounds, yet still could not hit the creature. Each round simply punched through the RV windshield. Maggie continued to scream they were both been flung helpless around inside of their steel trap. Dary, desperately trying to brace himself against the oven, took aim again, and fired the last two shots, still missing arm that was groping and grabbing frantically inside the RV.

Thirty minutes, later, which seemed like an eternity to Daryl and Maggie, the sheriff's vehicle had arrived at the rest are. The sound of approaching sheriffs vehicle's siren grew louder and louder as they got closer. The creature, upon hearing the sirens of the sheriff's cars, turned and ran back into the woods.

The two deputies cautiously approached the RV.

"Police, come out with your hands up!" yelled Deputy Feltzer.

After waiting for nearly ten minutes, the deputies stormed the RV, hoping to find a mad gunmen, but instead found Daryl holding his injured wife. Feltzer, after assessing the woman's injury, immediately called for paramedics.

"Daryl, can you describe the man that attacked you?" asked Deputy Feltzer.

"Man? Uhh . . . we're not sure that it was a man!" said Daryl.

"Can you explain what you mean?" asked Feltzer.

"Maggie, was it a man?" Daryl asked.

"I don't know what it was!" she replied.

"Feltzer, look what I found!" yelled Deputy Clay.

Feltzer came up the entrance of the vehicle, which had been force open, as if someone tried to sqeeze a refridgerator through the opening.

"Feltzer, it looks like long hair . . . and blood. Ma'am, is this your hair on the entrance where the door used to be?" asked Clay. "No, my hair is not that long." Maggie replied.

"Clay, take some samples for the crime lab!" said Feltzer.

"Sir, tell me what you saw!" said Feltzer.

"It was big and hairy!" said Daryl.

"Was it a bear that pulled the door off of your vehicle?" asked Feltzer.

"No. I don't think it was a bear!" said Daryl.

"Then it was a person! What did he look like?" asked Feltzer. "I don't know. Wait, I said didn't say it was a man!" said Daryl. "Then what attacked you?" asked Feltzer, with obvious confusion on his face.

"We don't know!" said Daryl.

"You said it was big and hairy?" asked Feltzer.

"Like an ape!" said Daryl.

"Maggie, was that an ape?" Daryl asked.

"I don't know what it was!" she replied.

The paramedics finally arrive, and unfortunately News Channel 7. Maggie was gingerly placed inside the ambulance. Daryl, sketched out what he thought he saw and handled the drawings to Feltzer.

"Feltzer, I've got tracks leading away from the RV!" yelled Clay. Deputy Feltzer stepped out of the RV and looked at the snow with Clay.

"Go get him! I'lls stay with the couple." said Feltzer.

Deputy Clay went to his squad car, and quickly came back with his shogun. He began following tracks within minutes, he was out of sight, still following the tracks.

"Camp 1, Delta 42" radioed Feltzer.

"Go ahead 42!" came the reply.

"I need two units plus K-9 at the King's Castle Rest Area." said Feltzer.

"10-4" came the reply.

Feltzer called Deputy Mills on his cellular phone.

"Mills, this is Feltzer. That guy in the monkey suit just attacked a couple at the King's Castle Rest Area!" said Feltzer.

"Really!" replied Deputy Mills.

"Now check this out! This time he was wearing a black monkey suit, not a gray one! This is a fine way to kick off opening week for Kings Castle, don't you think?" laughed Feltzer.

Chapter 19

Black Valley
Reservation

"**M**om that was a good dinner you cooked!" complimented Julie Blackhawk.

Her mother just smiled in reply from across the table. Julie picked up the dinner plates, glasses, and remaining food and carried them all back to the kitchen while her mother sat on the sofa and resumed work on her quilt. Julie's mother was well-known in several different tribal communities for her craftsmanship in quilt-making. She had sold dozens of quilts in the past, all of them for a premium price due to the high quality and beauty. She had been working on this quilt for nearly three months, and finally it was nearly finished. This quilt in particular was the most intricate one she had every made. The quilt had an elaborate and intricate design of the sun, the river in the valley, the eagle, and the bear. The quilt expressed in certain ways the depth, richness, and mystery of her tribe. This quilt, however, would not be for sale, but was to be to be passed down to her grandchildren. She felt that a quilt would be the best way to preserve the memory of her and also the memory of her tribe's culture.

As Julie Blackhawk had finished rinsing the last cup, she suddenly had an eerie feeling that she had never experienced in all her life. Julie felt as though there was someone or something watching her from outside of the window. She looked out her kitchen window and only saw the white, snow-covered, hilly landscape and dense evergreen forest, and falling snow. She looked up into the sky, hoping to see the stars, but instead saw the dense clouds, illuminated from behind by a full moon. After a few moments, she discarded the strange feeling as nothing more than just a fleeting, silly thought. After finishing the dishes, Julie walked to the living room to see how her mother was progressing with the quilt. Her mother was still busy knitting the quilt and watching the evening news.

"Would you like some coffee, Mom?" Julie gently asked. "Yes, please." her mother smiled. Julie walked back into the kitchen and reached for the pot, which had just finished brewing. Suddenly Julie noticed a faint smell in the air. The smell was faint, but terrible.

Hmmm . . . where did that smell come from? she thought to herself. Julie came back and gladly handed the fresh coffee to her mother.

"Mom, do you smell something?" Julie asked.

"Ummm . . . now that you mentioned it, I do smell something." her mother replied. The two women went to the kitchen to investigate the source of the smell. Julie proceeded to open all the cabinets on both sides of the window, to see if she might be able to discover anything that might account for the odor. After removing several stacks of plates, and searching under the sink. Julie's mother said, "Well, I thought maybe we'd find a dead mouse or something, but everything appears to be normal."

"Mother the smell is getting stronger!" said Julie."Could it be the sink?" asked Julie. Julie's mother sniffed the area around the sink, thinking that the smell might be coming from the drain

"The smell is not coming from the drain." said Julie's mother. "There's nothing in the cabinets." said Julie.

"I think it's coming from the window." her mother said.

"Mom the smells getting stronger!" said Julie.

"Open the window and see if it's coming from outside." said Julie's mother.

Julie opened the window. A blast of cold winter wind rushed into the kitchen, carry some snow it.

"The smell is coming from outside! I can't tell what it is?" said Julie. Suddenly they heard the snapping of branches or twigs coming from the direction of the back down. Julie ran to the back door and moved the door's curtain aside to peer out into the backyard. Immediately Julie noticed, in the distance, two tall, gigantic, shaggy figures approaching the boundary of the back yard. Horror filled Julie as she immediately identified the figures, both nearly twice as tall as a human. The figures black bodies were silhouetted in the moonlight, against the white backgrounds. Their faces could not be seen, but their were undoubtedly alive and walking towards the house. Julie screamed.

"Mom! Mom! They're coming!" Julie screamed.

"What? Who's coming?" replied her mother.

"Lamaniki!" exclaimed Julie, as she locked the deadbolt on the back door, and walked backwards to her mother. Both women, filled with terror, stood holding each other as the sound of crunching snow got closer to the back door. Julie's mother pulled the phone off of the counter and called 911. "Police, how can I help you?" came the voice of the desk officer.

"Lamaniki!" screamed Julie's mother, as she dropped the phone onto the counter. Suddenly there was a violent impact on the back door, so intense that it rattled the walls and sent wall portraits flying to the floor. Another impacted shattered the door window sending glass onto the floor at their feet. A deafening ghoulish wail filled the house as the creature began to pull on the door. The walls began to shake violently as the creature pulled and shook the door. Suddenly the door was ripped off its hinges. The creature stuck his massive, black, nightmarish head into the door and wailed as it looked at the two screaming women. The creature tried desperately to enter the door, but its massively broad shoulders wouldn't permit it to squeeze through. It began to violent shake in an effort to enter the house. The creature was tightly lodged in the door way. The violent twisting and turning motions of the creatures caused the walls to rattle. Paint chips, portraits, and decorative articles fell off of the wall as the creature continued its violent efforts to squeeze into the house. The house was newly constructed of cinder blocks and amazingly withstood the violent twisting and turning of the creature's body. Suddenly, directly behind the screaming women, there was a violent crashed heard. The two women looked around to see the front door shake with each unknown blow. The front door rattled uncontrollable as some unseen force acted on it. Over and over again something continued to smash against it. Suddenly the front door was also ripped off of its hinges. Another huge beast thrusted it's black ugly into the door. Upon seeing the two women inside, it also yelled out a deafening angry roar. Julie's mother fainted at the site of the second creature. She fell like a heavy sack towards the floor. She hit the floor hard before Julie had the chance to catch her falling body.

The determined creatures vainly tried to squeeze their way into the house, but neither could fit through the door frames.

Fortunately for women, their cinderblock house was able to keep the beasts out. For a hellish ten minutes the two monsters vainly continued to reach in and squeeze through the doors. Julie could do nothing more than scream, hold her mother, and stare at the two monsters that were desperately tried to reach for them. Each wailing cry of the monster sent shivers of terror up Julie's spine.

Suddenly Julie noticed the red and blue emergency lights flashing in the blackness of night. Two Indian police officers jumped out and began firing at the creature that was wedged in the front door. The creature, feelings the rounds hit its back quickly backed out of the front door, and made its way toward the officers. One officer continued to fire repeatedly with his sidearm, while the other officer fired buckshot. The officers were baffled as they notice that their weapons did seem to affect the oncoming animal.

"Get back into the car!" yelled the senior officer. The men jumped back into the car.

"Fasten your seat belt!" the he yelled.

The officer put the car in reverse and slowly pulled the vehicle back about twenty yards. The creature followed the police vehicle.

"Good, good, come and get it!" said the driver.

As soon as the creature came up to the front of the vehicle, the driver placed the vehicle in drive and drove around the creature. The officer drive up the house placing the passengers doors of the police vehicle as close as he could to the front door of the house.

"Go get the ladies!" the officer yelled his partner. The second officer ran in and scooped Julie's mother off of the floor. The officer and Julie ran out of the house and to the car. As carefully as the officer could he placed Julie's mother into the back of the car, and then helped Julie get into the back of the car.

"Hurry! Hurry!" screamed the driver. The creature that was in the backyard, then made his way around the side of the house. Just as the second officer jumped in, the other creature had made its way to the front door and approached the police car from the front, at the same time the other creature closed in from the driver's side.

The officer placed the car in reverse to increase the distance between the car and the marauding beasts. He then hit the gas pedal and sped in between the two creatures, narrowly missing both creatures. The creature nearest the driver's side desperately reached for the police car and grabbed the emergency equipment. In so doing, the creature ripped the emergency lights off of the top of the car as the car sped away. The officer picked reached for the car's radio and dialed in to the sheriff's channel.

"Sherriff's Dispatch . . . Bureau of Indians Police!" he called. "Go ahead Indian Police." came the reply.

"We need back up units at the Black Valley Reservation!" "What is the emergency?" asked Sheriff's dispatch. "Umm . . . animal attack! Request backup!" replied the police officer.

"10-4 . . . Do we have any units that could rendezvous with Indian Police at the reservation?" asked Sheriff's dispatch.

"Unit 35 enroute, ETA thirty minutes!" said one deputy.

"Unit 52 ETA thirty minutes!" came another reponse.

"Unit 90 . . . forty five minutes!" came a third answer. The Indian Police officers knew that it would be more than thirty minutes, due to the remoteness of the reservation and its distance from the highway.

The Indian police car made its way through the winding snow-covered dirt road, along the valley floor towards the front gate. Under the best of conditions, the trip from Julie's house to the gate office would take a minimum of twenty minutes. It was just sheer chance that the men were patrolling near Julie's solitary house.

Julie's mother awoke and screamed. "It's okay, Mom, we're in the police car!" said Julie reassuringly, holding her mother tightly. The car finally reached the gate office and they entered into the warm building.

Chapter 20

Ricky and Jake

One a cold, snowy morning, the U.S. Forest Service helicopter left the helipad at 7:00 a.m., carry Ricky and the pilot.

"What's your first name?" asked Ricky.

"Jake." the pilot replied.

"And yours?" asked Jake.

"Ricky. Pleased to meet you!" replied Ricky.

"Where are we going, Sir?" asked Jake.

"We are going to see the wreckage of that private helicopter that went down a few days ago, but that will be on our second trip, if we don't find anything on our first trip." replied Ricky. "Oh yeah . . . I remember hearing about. Do you think we'll find that beast?" asked Jake. Ricky was surprised as he looked out of the window in front of him. *How did Jake know about the monster? Well, I guess the secret is no longer a secret! The whole world knows that we got a monster on the loose!* Ricky thought to himself.

"Who knows? Probably not, but it's worth a look." smiled Ricky.

"How many shotgun slugs did you bring?" asked Jake, staring at the shotgun Ricky had in his hand.

"Ten. I hope it'll be enough." replied Ricky. After a beautiful, calm, fifteen minute flight through the mountains, they arrived to the area where the helicopter that carried Troy had crashed. They circled the area for a while. Ricky scanned the area through his binoculars until his eyes were tired. Finally the pilot notified him that they were low and fuel and had to return to the base. They returned to the station and rested in the station's cantina to drink coffee while the helicopter was being refueled. Ricky called Rusty Gaines."Mr. Gaines, we found nothing on the first flight. If it alright with you, we are going out again." said Ricky.

"Have at it!" replied Gaines.

"Ready to out again?" asked Ricky.

"Ready if you are!" smiled Jake. On this second flight Ricky intended to scan a different part of the mountain range, in the opposite direction, farther west, from the Big Flower Convenience store. After another long flight, the two arrived at the peak where the deputies had lost the creature's footprints. They circled the peak a few times looking for anything that resembled a footprint or any signs of any disturbance among the trees and branches. After while, Jake said, "We getting low on fuel, we need to return to the station, soon."

"No problem." replied Ricky. Suddenly a movement caught Jake's eye.

"Ricky, what was that?"

"What was what?" asked Ricky.

155

"I saw some kind of movement, right over there!" replied Jake. Ricky looked down in the direction that Jake was pointing, but saw nothing but the snow-covered tree tops.

"Put the helicopter down where you saw it!" replied Ricky. Jake quickly turned the helicopter around and proceeded to land in area where he saw the moving object. He then brought the helicopter down into a large clearing in a deep ravine, guarded on both sides by large boulders and dense, snow-covered evergreens. Jake brought the helicopter to a hover at about twenty feet about the ground.

"I saw something moving right in front of us, behind those tall trees."

"What color was it?" asked Ricky.

"I'm not sure! It was really big and it was moving!" replied Jake.

"Let's go get it! Can you set us down so we don't burn anymore fuel? Can we still make it back to the base!" asked Ricky.

"Yeah, we should be fine on fuel. I always announce fuel quantity on the conservative side just to be safe. I'll put us down." said Jake. Within a minute, the helicopter was down on a clearing, in the middle of the ravine.

"Camp 1 . . . Echo 9!" radioed Ricky.

"Go for Camp 1!" came the reply from the communications center.

"Show us landed 1.2 miles west of the Big Flower Convenience Store on HWY 94. We are in the fifth ravine from the convenience store. We'll be patrolling the area." said Ricky.

"Fifth ravine, 10-4!" came the reply.

"Jake, do you have a gun?"

"No, I'm just a pilot. I'm not licensed to carry one." replied Jake.

"No problem, I have this extra 1911 on me. Hold onto it. I won't tell anyone if you don't!" said Ricky, as he handed the pistol to him.

"Pistol? What pistol!" grinned Jake, as he slid the gun into his pocket.

"Do you know how to use a 1911?" asked Ricky.

"I already own one just like it!" replied Jake.

"Here, put these two bottles of water in your jacket, in case we are in for a little hike." said Ricky.

"Thanks." said Jake. Both men jumped out of the helicopter and ran forward to the dense cluster of tall pine trees. Upon arriving at the trees, the sign of massive eighteen inch clawed footprints was immediately noticeable.

Jake's eyes bulged as he stared at the massive footprints. "I knew I saw something . . . and it wasn't a bear!"

"Do a press check!" said Ricky. Both men drew out their pistols and pulled the slide back just far enough to ensure that there was a round already in the chamber. Ricky racked the slide on his shot gun, chambering a one ounce slug. Ricky sniffed the air, hoping to notice that reeking stench he noticed during his first encounter with the creature. He sniffed continually for several minutes, but noticed nothing.

"Do you smell anything?" asked Ricky.

"What should I be smelling for?" asked Jake.

"Anything strong, anything really bad." replied Ricky.

Jake took a few sniffs. "I don't notice anything." What they didn't realize was that the wind was blowing the smell of the creature away from them.

"Alright then, let's try to follow these tracks." said Ricky. The men followed the massive foot prints further down the snowy ridge.

"I can't believe this! All along I doubted the stories of this kind of creature!" said Jake.

"So did I until I saw it. I'm out here because I've got to stop it from killing more people." said Ricky.

"What? You saw it?" asked Jake.

"It broke my ribs and took my horse from underneath me." said Ricky.

"No kidding!" replied Jake. The two men continued to follow the footprints down the steep ravine for another fifteen minutes.

"Watch your step, these rocks are icy and slick." warned Ricky. Before Ricky could finish speaking, Jake had slipped and found himself flat on his back against the rocks.

"Yeah, I noticed." replied Jake, as Ricky helped him to his feet. The men made it to the bottom of the ravine where they met a dense forest of tall, snow-covered trees.

"The footprints clearly went into there!" said Ricky. Suddenly Jake started to notice a faint smell.

"Do you smell that?" asked Jake. Ricky stopped walking and took a deep breath. Jake was right; there was a barely noticeable stench in the area in from of them, coming from somewhere. It was same stench he noticed during his first encounter with the creature. Suddenly, Ricky realized that he was being overwhelmed with fear. He began to tremble with fear. How embarrassing!

I hope Jake doesn't notice me shaking like this! he thought to himself.

"Uh oh, now we're in trouble! Jake, that's the same stink I smelled when I met the creature!" replied Ricky.

"Jake?" Ricky stopped talking when he looked over and noticed Jake trembling uncontrollably in fear. Both men looked at each other and just laughed. Ricky raised his police shotgun to hip level firing position. Upon seeing this, Jake immediate drew out his pistol and pointed it forward.

"Jake, as soon as you see anything, shoot it till if falls to the ground, because it's not going to just look at us and walk away and it's not gonna be merciful to us!" said Ricky.

"Thanks for making me feel more at ease!" replied Jake. The men slowly and cautiously followed the footprints in between the dense trees and across large cap rocks. As the stench in the air was getting stronger, Ricky's fear intensified, causing him to tremble. Ricky tried desperately to control himself, but was having trouble keeping the shotgun steady. Ricky's fear heightened so much that he couldn't control the shaking in his arms and legs. The movement at the end of the shotgun's barrel gave away his nervousness. Ricky was getting embarrassed that he couldn't control himself. Ricky felt a little relief when he looked beside him to discover that Jake was also trembling with fear.

"Don't be ashamed! I'm shaking in my boots too!" said Jake. The men continued to follow the footprints through the dense forest. The footprints were winding left and right around the pines.

"Which direction are we facing now?" asked Ricky.

"After all that winding around we just did, I don't know anymore!" said Jake. To their dismay, the tracks ended at a cliff's edge, which dropped down perhaps fifty feet. Both men stood at the cliff's edge, which narrowed to a ten-feet wide area, and looked down towards the rocky bottom.

"Careful! Don't fall!" said Ricky.

"It couldn't have jumped down that far, could it?" asked Jake.

"How should I know? I think it's still nearby. I can still smell it!" replied Ricky.

"Yeah, I smell it too!" reply Jake.

"I'm getting tired of holding this pistol out in front of me." said Jake.

"You think that's heavy? Try holding this shotgun up for fifteen minutes!" laughed Ricky. What they didn't realize is that the creature knew that it was being followed. When it reached the cliff's edge, it climbed up the rocks, made a U-turn, and walked around them without leaving any footprints. The creature had circled around them nearly five minutes earlier and was now stalking them from behind! The men stood at the cliff's edge and continued looking at the steep drop off, trying to see the any tracks or usable path leading down to the bottom of the cliff. Ricky pulled out his binoculars to scan the steep area in front of him, hoping to see some tracks or at least some kind of movement.

"Jake, I don't get it. How did it make it down this cliff without leaving some kind of sign? Can you see any narrow trail or path of any sort?" asked Ricky.

"I'm still looking. It is just a sheer rocky drop off." replied Jake. The light wind changed direction and was now blowing directly into the men's faces as they stared over the cliff, drawing the creature's smell away from them. The creature slowly came out from the trees, seventy yards directly behind them, without making a sound. Suddenly the creature roared and made a mad dash at them. The men turned around in horror at the sound of its voice, and saw the massive shaggy figure barreling down on them, without it clawed hands outstretched. The men were in a precarious position, having the cliff behind them and the creature in front of them. "Shoot it!" shouted Ricky. Within seconds Jake had emptied the eight round magazine of the pistol, as Ricky also sent off slug rounds. The creature only flinched once as it was hit in its chest by a slug, yet it continued to run towards the men. Not knowing that he had emptied the shotgun, Ricky pulled the trigger only to hear the sound of the hammer falling on empty chamber. Click! The hammer of the shotgun hit an empty chamber. Ricky felt a wave of panic shoot through his body. Ricky looked around him in desperation and noticed a thick patch of evergreen trees, just below him.

"Jump, jump, it's getting too close!" screamed Ricky.

"Jump? Jump where?" demanded Jake.

"Into the tree tops! We can't climb down the rocks!" yelled Ricky, as he jumped. Both men turned and jumped to the left and fell nearly ten feet into the tops of snow covered trees. Both men used their arms to shield their faces and chest, and braced for the impact. The men crashed through the top branches, snapping all of them, and continue to crash downward through all of the branches. Breaking halfway down the trees, the branches became thicker and bounced the men around until they finally hit the snowy bottom. Jack sustained two broken ribs and lacerations on the side of his head. Ricky also received multiple lacerations on his forehead and received a broken nose when his face hit that last branch coming down. Ricky's torso was unharmed due to the ballistics vest he was wearing. Both men lay momentarily at the base of the trees. Ricky lay still for a moment looking up at the cloudy sky and tree tops. He began to feel his legs, arms, and chest for signs of broken bones. When he felt his face, it felt that it was warm and wet. He looked at his hands and saw that they were covered with blood. His broken nose was bleeding profusely. He was also bleeding from his mouth, where he bit his lip when he was being bounced between the branches. He looked over to Jake, who was lying in the snow near him. Jake was wheezing with great difficulty and was in obvious pain.

"It's my chest! Uh oh. this doesn't feel right!" said Jake. Ricky crawled over and unzipped Ricky's coat to discover and abnormal looking lumps underneath Jakes polo shirt around the ribs.

"Ricky, you've got blood all over your face!" said Jake.

"I know . . . I can taste it!" Ricky replied. The blood from Ricky's nose and forehead dripped onto the snow next to Jake as Ricky looked at the unnatural lumps protruding from Jakes shirt.

"Jake, it looks like you've got one or more broken ribs." Ricky said. Both men had temporarily forgotten about the creature until it roared again. Ricky looked frantically around for the shotgun. It was nowhere to be found!

"Where's the gun I handed you?" asked Ricky.

"I don't know. I had it a second ago." replied Jake. Ricky looked around for the shotgun, but it was lost in the fall. Fortunately, for Ricky, his sidearm was still locked in his triple retention holster. He quickly jumped up and pulled out his pistol, looking in every direction for any signs of movement. Ricky reached for his radio.

"Camp 1, Echo 9" called Ricky.

"Go for Camp 1" came the reply from dispatch.

"Request LifeLine helicopter, thirty minutes west of Big Flower Convenience Store also additional Airborne Mobility Rangers with long arms for rescue operation."

"10-4! Do you have GPS coordinates?" asked dispatch. "Negative. We are approximately 1.2 miles west of the convenience store plus 30 minutes westward on foot, at the bottom of the rock waterfall.

"Good copy! Will dispatch LifeLine and also additional rangers." replied dispatch. Ricky knew that it would be at least twenty minutes for help to arrive. *That's twenty minutes too long!* he thought to himself.

The creature roared again. Judging by the sound of it, it was still somewhere above them. Ricky quickly paced the area around them, trying to locate the shotgun in the snow. He still had five additional rounds in his pocket, and wanted to use them before resorting to his pistol. The creature roared again. This time the sound came from a different direction. "Jake, it's on its way down!" Ricky said. Ricky continued to scurry around to find that shotgun. Suddenly he spotted the shotgun nearly twenty yards away, nearly completely buried in the snow. He ran for it. As soon as he pulled it out of the snow, he spotted the creature above him. The creature slowly continued to step downward across the icy rocks and tree roots. Ricky decided not to look behind him, thus giving away the location of his wounded companion. As quickly as he could, he loaded the last five slugs into the shotgun. By the time he load the last slug, the creature had made its way down to the clearing where the men were and was about twenty meters in front of him. Ricky racked the slide and took aim at the creature's center mass. *Boom!* The slug missed altogether. Ricky fired another round. The second slug smashed into the creature's chest, and to Ricky's surprise, knocked it backwards to the ground. The creature wailed in pain, but immediately stood up and continued its advance upon Ricky. Ricky's jaw dropped as he looked at the oncoming creature in disbelief. He decided to go for a head shot. He racked the slide again and fired. The slug flew past the creature's head. He racked the slide a fourth time and fired. The slug slammed into the chest near the first hole, sending the creature backwards to the ground again. Like before, the creature wailed, but immediate got up and advanced, again. Ricky racked the last slug and aim for the creatures face. *Boom!* The slug ripped the ear off of the creature's head. It simply flinched, roared, and continued walking closer, with its arms outstretched. Ricky dropped to one knee, dropped the shotgun, and punched out with his pistol. He fired desperately at the creature's head, missing every shot. Finally the last round, locking the pistol's slide open, found its target. It penetrated the creature's right eye and sent shards of large skull fragments into the creature's tiny brain. The pistol round could not penetrate the back of the skull, but simply lodged into it. As Ricky skillfully performed and emergency pistol reload, the creature fell forward like a massive tree and crashed into the snow, just a few feet in front of Ricky. As the creature hit the ground, it sent snow in every direction, including into Ricky's face. Ricky remained in the kneeling position, shaking uncontrollably, with his aim still fixed in the direction of the monster.

Both Ricky and Jake remained still, and stared at the shaggy mass for several minutes.

"You did it!" yelled Jake, exuberantly. "Uh . . . yuh . . . yuh . . . yuh . . . yeah." stammered Ricky.

Twenty minutes later, the sound of two helicopters could be heard in the distance. Within minutes, two EMTs and three Air Mobility Rangers were on scene to assist them.

"You killed the monster that nearly killed you before!" exclaimed Jake. Ricky slowly stood to his feet, shaking in fear, and slowly walked backwards away from the creature. "No I didn't. This one is black. The one that attacked me . . . was ash gray." he replied.